"Merry...short for Meredith," Kimberly mused

"Is that what your friends call you?"

Meredith hesitated, glancing quickly at Nick Hamilton. "Only one other person has ever used that name for me."

There was almost a savage, primitive satisfaction in relating who it had been, knowing that Nick Hamilton was listening, unaware she was speaking of him. "It was your father, Kimberly. Your real father. When he met me he said it was like all the Christmas lights in the world switched on inside him."

Suddenly she choked, the memory so vivid, and here she was, all these years later, sitting with the heart-wrenching outcome of the one love affair of her life...with a daughter she didn't know and the lover who didn't know her.

Initially a French/English teacher, *EMMA DARCY* changed careers to computer programming before marriage and motherhood settled her into a community life. Creative urges were channeled into oil painting, pottery, designing and overseeing the construction and decorating of two homes, all in the midst of keeping up with three lively sons and the very social life of her businessman husband, Frank. Very much a people person and always interested in relationships, she finds the world of romance fiction a happy one and the challenge of creating her own cast of characters very addictive. She enjoys traveling, and her experiences often find their way into her books. Emma Darcy lives on a country property in New South Wales, Australia.

Books by Emma Darcy

HARLEQUIN PRESENTS
1833—THE FATHER OF HER CHILD
1848—THEIR WEDDING DAY
1857—JACK'S BABY
1881—CRAVING JAMIE
1900—MARRIAGE MELTDOWN
1906—SEDUCING THE ENEMY

and in MIRA Books
THE SECRETS WITHIN

Don't miss any of our special offers. Write to us at the following address for information on our newest releases.

Harlequin Reader Service
U.S.: 3010 Walden Ave., P.O. Box 1325, Buffalo, NY 14269
Canadian: P.O. Box 609, Fort Erie, Ont. L2A 5X3

EMMA DARCY

Merry Christmas

Harlequin Books

TORONTO • NEW YORK • LONDON
AMSTERDAM • PARIS • SYDNEY • HAMBURG
STOCKHOLM • ATHENS • TOKYO • MILAN
MADRID • WARSAW • BUDAPEST • AUCKLAND

ISBN 0-373-11923-2

MERRY CHRISTMAS

First North American Publication 1997.

This edition published by arrangement with Harlequin Books S.A.

® and TM are trademarks of the publisher. Trademarks indicated with ® are registered in the United States Patent and Trademark Office, the Canadian Trade Marks Office and in other countries.

Printed in U.S.A.

CHAPTER ONE

"UNCLE NICK? You asked me what I want for Christmas?"

Kimberly's belligerent tone was forewarning enough that Nick was not going to like it. His twelve-year-old niece could be as difficult and as trying as a fully fledged teenager. She'd been sulking in her room ever since Rachel had arrived for Sunday brunch and this sudden, dramatic challenge, fired at him from the doorway to the balcony, was not a promise of peace and harmony. The plot, he deduced, was to demand something totally unreasonable and stir contention.

"Mmmh?" he said non-committally, staying behind his newspaper in the hope of taking the sting out of the bait.

Rachel's newspaper rustled down. Undoubtedly she was looking at Kimberly with a brightly encouraging smile, doing her best to win the girl over. An increasingly futile exercise, Nick thought gloomily.

"I want my *real* mother."

The shock of it almost wiped him out. The wallop to his heart took some absorbing and his mind totally fused. Fortunately his hands went into clench mode, keeping the newspaper up in cover defence while the initial impact of the surprise attack gave way to fast and furious thought.

Her *real* mother…was it a try-on, a fantasy, or sure knowledge? Impossible to tell without looking at her. He composed his face into an expression of puzzled inquiry and lowered his newspaper.

"I beg your pardon?"

Fierce green eyes scorned his bluff. "*You* know, Uncle Nick. The solicitor would have told you when Mum and Dad died. You couldn't have become my legal guardian without knowing."

Still he played it warily. "What am I supposed to know, Kimberly?"

"That I was adopted."

Absolute certainty looked him straight in the face. It threw Nick into confusion. Kimberly was not supposed to know. His sister had been almost paranoid about keeping the secret. After the fatal accident last year, Nick had thought it best to keep the knowledge from his niece until she was eighteen. After all, losing both parents in traumatic circumstances and learning to live with an uncle was a big enough adjustment to make. Any further erosion of her sense of security did not seem a good idea.

"I have a *real* mother," came the vehement assertion, her chin tilting defiantly, her eyes flashing resentment at Rachel before pinning Nick again. "I want to be with *her* for Christmas."

He folded the newspaper and set it aside, realising this confrontation was very serious, indeed. 'How long have you known, Kimberly?" he asked quietly.

"Ages," she tossed at him.

"Who told you?" It had to be Colin, he thought. His sister's husband had been a gentle man, dominated by Denise for the most part, yet retaining an innate personal dignity and integrity that would not be shaken over matters he considered "right."

"No one told me," Kimberly answered loftily. "I figured it out for myself."

That rocked him. Had he conceded confirmation too soon? Too easily? How on earth could Kimberly figure it out for herself?

If someone had actually worked at matching a child to a family to ensure an adopted baby looked like natural offspring, Kimberly would be a prime example of outstanding success. She could easily be claimed by his side of the family.

She was long-legged and tall, like himself and his sister. Her black hair had the same springy texture and she even had a widow's peak hairline, a family feature that went back generations. The eye colour—green instead of brown—was easily explained with Colin's eyes being hazel. There were untraceable differences—every person was uniquely individual—but if his sister had declared her adopted child her own flesh and blood, Nick would never have doubted it.

So why had Kimberly?

"Would you mind telling me what gave it away to you?" he asked, trying to keep his voice calmly controlled.

"The photographs," she said as though throwing down irrefutable proof.

Nick had no idea what she was talking about.

She flounced forward and picked a cherry off the fruit platter he and Rachel had been sharing, popped it into her mouth and ostentatiously chewed it, hugging her budding chest, aggressively holding the floor, waiting for him to comment. Her green eyes had a fighting gleam.

Rebellion was in the air, from the swing of her ponytail to the brightly checked orange-yellow shorts teamed with a lime green tank top. Kimberly was making statements; right, left and centre. She was not going to be ignored, overlooked or left in the wings of anybody's life.

Nick glanced at Rachel who had tactfully withdrawn any obvious interest in the family contretemps. From the balcony of his Blues Point apartment, one could take in a vast sweep of Sydney Harbour. Rachel's gaze was fixed on the water view but her stillness revealed an acute listening and suddenly Nick didn't want her hearing this, despite their intimate relationship.

"Rachel, this is a very private family matter..."

"Of course." She rose quickly from her chair, flashing him an understanding smile. "I'll let myself out and leave you to it, Nick."

There was so much about Rachel he liked...very capable, highly intelligent, shrewdly perceptive about most people, though his twelve-year-old niece frequently flummoxed her. Even their careers dovetailed, she an investment advisor, he a banker. They were both in their thirties. As a prospective partner in life, Rachel Pearce looked about as good as Nick thought he was going to get, desirable in every sense, yet...the magic connection was missing.

As she stood up, sunshine glinted off her auburn hair, turning the short hairstyle into a glorious, copper cap. Good-looking, always chic, sexy, comfortable with men, her sherry brown eyes invariably warm for him... Nick wondered what more he could want in a woman?

Nevertheless, it didn't feel right for her to be privy to such sensitive family secrets as Kimberly's adoption. It involved delving into lives that only he and his niece had known and shared. It was not Rachel's business. Not yet.

He rose from his chair at the same time, intent on taking command of the situation. "Thanks for your company, Rachel."

"My pleasure. I hope..." She glanced at Kimberly who was helping herself to another cherry, stiffly and steadfastly ignoring her, then with a last rueful look at Nick, she shrugged her helplessness and turned to leave.

"Even if my real mother doesn't want me, I won't go to your old boarding school anyway," Kimberly shot after her. "So you needn't think you can get rid of me that easily."

Rachel froze in the doorway to the living room.

Nick's heart sustained another breathtaking blow. His mind, however, did have something to clutch on to this time—his conversation with Rachel last night. Kimberly should have been in her room asleep but she must have eavesdropped. This current mood and stance had clearly been fermenting ever since.

"It's not a matter of getting rid of you, Kimberly," he said tersely. "It's a matter of what's best for you."

"You mean what's best for you," she retorted. "And best for her." Her eyes flared fierce resentment. "I'm not stupid, Uncle Nick."

"Precisely. Which is why I'd like you to start your secondary education at a good school. To give you the best teachers and the best education."

"Most girls would consider it a privilege to go to PLC," Rachel argued with some heat. "It's certainly been advantageous to me."

"Well, you would say that, wouldn't you?" Kimberly retaliated. "Anything to shunt me out of the way. You think I don't know when I'm not wanted?"

"That's enough, Kimberly," Nick warned. Rachel had tried to reach out to his niece. There just didn't seem to be any meeting place. Or she wasn't granted one.

"Why boarding school, Uncle Nick?" came the pointed challenge. "If it's only education you're thinking of, why couldn't I go as a day pupil? PLC is right here in Sydney."

"You're on your own too much, Kimberly," he answered. "I thought the companionship of other girls would round out your life more."

"*You* thought?" An accusing glare at Rachel. "Or Ms. Pearce suggested?"

"I was going to discuss it with you after Christmas."

The accusative glare swung onto him. "You told her to go ahead and try to get me in."

"That's still not decisive, Kimberly. And you shouldn't have been eavesdropping."

"If Mum had wanted me to go to an expensive, private boarding school, she would have booked me in years ago." Tears glittered in her eyes. "You don't want me. Not like Mum and Dad did."

The recognition of unresolved grief was swift and sharp. His stomach clenched. He couldn't replace her parents. No one could. He missed them, too, his only sibling who'd virtually brought him up, and Colin who'd always given him affectionate support and approval. It had been a struggle this past year, trying to merge his life with a twelve-year-old's, but not once had he begrudged the task or the responsibility.

"I do want you, Kimberly," he assured her gravely.

She shook her head, her face screwing up with conflicting and painful emotions. "I was dumped on you and now you want to dump me somewhere else."

"No."

She swiped her eyes with the back of her hand, smearing the wetness aside. "You won't have to do anything if my real mother wants me. You can give me up and have your lady friend free and clear of somebody else's daughter." She glared balefully at Rachel. "I don't want to be stuck with you any more than you want to be stuck with me, Ms. Pearce."

Rachel heaved a sigh and rolled her eyes at Nick, powerless to stop the hostility aimed at her.

"Just go, Rachel," he advised quietly.

"Sorry, Nick."

"Not your fault."

"No, it's my fault," Kimberly cried, her voice rising toward shrill hysteria. "I spoil it for both of you. So I'm the one who should go."

The arm Nick swung out to stop her was left hanging uselessly as she rushed to the doorway and ducked past Rachel into the living room. He swiftly followed her but she ran full pelt to the front door, pausing only to yell back at him.

"If you care anything at all about me, Uncle Nick, you'll do it. You'll get my *real* mother for me for Christmas! Then maybe it could turn out right for all of us."

CHAPTER TWO

IT HADN'T come today, either...the letter from Denise Graham with news of Kimberly and the photographs spanning another year.

Meredith Palmer struggled to fight off a depressing wave of anxiety as she entered her apartment and locked the rest of the world out. Again she shuffled through the stack of mail she'd just collected from her box; Christmas cards, bank statement, an advertising brochure. She opened the envelopes and extracted the contents, making doubly sure there was no mistake. Nothing from Denise Graham.

The packet usually came in the last week of November. It had done so for the past eleven years. Today was the fourteenth of December and the uneasy feeling that something was wrong was fast growing into conviction. Denise Graham had come across to Meredith, even in her letters, as a very precise person, the kind who would live by a strictly kept timetable. Unless the packet had somehow been lost or misdirected in the volume of Christmas mail, something had to be badly wrong in the Graham household.

Illness? An accident?

The tight feeling in her chest grew tighter as disastrous possibilities flew through Meredith's mind. Not Kimberly, she fiercely prayed. Please...not Kimberly. Her little girl had to have a wonderful life ahead of her. Only by believing that had Meredith managed to repress the misery of not having kept her daughter.

She shook her head, fighting back the worst-case scenarios. Maybe something had happened to the solicitor who had handled the legal aspects of the adoption and subsequently become a conduit for the annual updates to Meredith. Whenever she'd had a change of address she had contacted him, at least half a dozen times before she'd saved enough money to invest in this apartment at Balmoral. Each time she had received a note of acknowledgment and nothing had gone wrong. Nevertheless, it could be that someone else was now handling his business, someone not as meticulously efficient.

She walked across her living room to the writing desk which spread across one corner, linking two walls of bookcases. Having automatically sorted her mail for future replies, she dropped it into inbaskets, then opened a drawer and took out her address book. It was too late to contact the firm of solicitors today but she'd do it first thing tomorrow. It made her feel better, simply copying the telephone number into the notebook she always carried in her handbag.

Despite having set herself a constructive course of action, Meredith still found it impossible to stop worrying. She switched on the television set to catch the evening news but didn't hear a word of it. The glass of white wine she poured herself was consumed although she had no conscious memory of drinking it. After opening the refrigerator and staring at the contents of the shelves for several minutes without connecting anything together for a proper meal, she gave up on the idea of cooking and settled on cheese and pickles and crackers.

The problem was, she didn't have a legal leg to stand on if Denise Graham had decided, for some reason, to break off the one promised contact with her. It had been a matter of trust, her letting Meredith know about their daughter's life once a year...one mother's word to another...an act of compassion in the face of Meredith's grief at giving up her baby. If the solicitor told her there was to be no more contact, there was nothing she could do about it. Absolutely nothing.

A sense of helplessness kept eating at her, robbing her of any appetite, distracting her from doing anything purposeful. When the doorbell rang, she almost didn't answer it. A check of her watch put the time at a few minutes past eight. She wasn't expecting anyone and wasn't in the mood to entertain a visitor. Only the thought of a neighbour in need prompted her to open the door.

Living alone had established automatic precautions. The security chain lock on the door only allowed an opening of a few centimetres. It was through this space—like a long crack in the fabric of time—Meredith saw the man she had never expected to see again.

His eyes caught hers, triggering the weird gush of feeling that only he had ever evoked...the wild whoosh from her heart to her head, like the sea washing into her ears, followed by a fountain of excitement shooting, splashing, rippling through her entire body, setting up an electric tingling of expectation for the most special connection in the world.

It had been like that for her thirteen years ago. As she stared at him now, the shocked sense of her world reeling backward was so strong, all she could do was stare and grip the doorknob with painful intensity, needing some reinforcement of current physical reality.

"Miss Palmer? Meredith Palmer?"

His voice struck old familiar chords that had lain dormant so long Meredith had forgotten them... chords of pleasure, of some sixth sense recognition, a deep resonant tone that thrummed through her, a seductive beat of belonging drawing on her soul.

Yet he didn't know her. She could see he didn't. He would have called her Merry. It had been his name for her...Merry...Merry Christmas...the best Christmas he had ever had.

"Yes," she said, affirming her identity, her heart

still bleeding over what his sister had sworn to her was the truth when she'd denied Meredith access to the father of her baby all those years ago. An accident had wiped out all memory of his summer vacation. He would have no recollection of her. Since he'd already left for the U.S. on a two-year study grant, Meredith had no possible way of testing if what his sister claimed was fact or fiction.

Now the evidence was in front of her. Not Merry. Miss Meredith Palmer with a question mark.

Yet shouldn't there be a gut memory? Shouldn't he feel at least an echo of what she was feeling? It hadn't been one-sided back in the summer of her sixteenth year.

"My name is Nick Hamilton..."

There was a pause, as though he had to regather his thoughts and concentrate them on his purpose for coming to her. Since it wasn't prompted by any memory of her—nerves tightened around Meredith's stomach—it had to be related to Kimberly. Had he found out Kimberly was his daughter? Had something happened to her? Was he the carrier of bad news from his sister?

"...I'm Denise Graham's brother," he stated, identifying the connection that gave him credentials for calling on her.

"Yes," Meredith repeated numbly, painfully aware of all the ramifications of that relationship. "You must have come about Kimberly. The packet..." She swallowed hard, a sickening wave of fear welling up over the emotional impact of seeing him again. "...I should have got it over a fortnight ago."

"So I understand," he said sympathetically. "May I come in? There's a lot to explain."

Meredith nodded, too choked up to speak. This man and his child had dominated the course of her life for thirteen years. To have him physically in front of her after all this time was both a dream and a nightmare. Her fingers fumbled over the chain slot. Her mind buzzed with the thought of letting him in...to far more than her apartment. And what of his child—her child—who had to be the reason he was here?

"Is Kimberly all right?" The question burst from her as she shakily drew the door wide for him to enter.

"Yes. Couldn't be healthier," came the quick assurance. He stepped inside, pausing beside her as she sagged in relief. His brow creased in concern and he made an apologetic gesture. "I'm sorry you were worried. Your daughter is fine, Miss Palmer."

The acknowledgment that she had a daughter brought tears to her eyes. No one in her current life knew. It had always been a painfully private part of her, not easily shared. Who could understand? There'd been so many forces pushing her into letting her baby go—for the best, they'd all said—but sometimes the mourning for the child she could never hold in her arms was overwhelming.

"Thank you," she managed huskily.

Agitated by Nick Hamilton's nearness, his understanding and his sympathy, she waved him on to her living room and made a prolonged business of relocking the door. Being situated on the fourth floor of this apartment building gave her some protection against break-ins and burglaries but Meredith was always careful. A woman on her own had to be in the city. Though it was impossible to protect against everything. She had opened her door and the past had rushed in on her tonight. Impossible to know at this point, whether it was good or bad.

"Nice place you have here."

The appreciative compliment strove to put this meeting on an ordinary footing. It almost provoked a hysterical laugh from Meredith. She took a deep breath, struggling to keep her wildly swinging emotions under control, then slowly turned to play gracious hostess to this gracious guest. Following a polite formula was probably the best way of coping with untenable dreams.

"Thank you," she said again, her voice steadier, more natural.

He stood mostly in profile, looking back at her from the end of the short hallway that led past the kitchenette to the living room. For a heart-catching moment she saw the twenty-two-year-old Nick Hamilton, as enraptured by her as she was by him, the air between them charged by a heightened awareness that excluded the rest of the world.

Her heart started to thump erratically. Stupid to think nothing had changed. He was still tall, dark and stunningly handsome, but his superb physique was now clothed in an executive-class suit, there were threads of silver in his glossy black hair, and the lines of his face had a mature set to them, harder, sharper, stronger. Life moved on. He was probably married. With other children.

She'd thought that thought a thousand times before, so why did it hurt like hell right now? Because he was here, she answered herself, and his eyes looked exactly the same as when he'd looked at her in the summertime of their youth, combining the slowly feasting sensuality of dark chocolate with the overlying shine of intense magnets, tugging on her soul.

But what was he seeing? She wasn't so young anymore, either, and she was suddenly acutely aware of her appearance. Her make-up was probably looking tired after the long day she'd put in at her office, mascara smudged under her eyes, lipstick faded to a pencilled outline. While her smooth olive skin didn't have blemishes to cover, the matt powder she used to reduce shine would have worn off.

Not exactly putting her best foot forward, she thought ruefully, and was instantly reminded she was standing in her stockinged feet, having kicked off her shoes when she'd come in. Not that it made much difference. She only ever wore little heels. Her legs were so long she always felt her tall, slim figure looked out of proportion in high heels. Nevertheless, the omission of shoes left her feeling even more ungroomed.

And her hair had to be adding to that impression. He'd once described it as strings of honeycomb and treacle—words of smiling whimsy. It was undoubtedly stringy tonight. It hadn't been brushed since this morning and it was so thick and fine it tended to look unkempt after a few hours, billowing out into a fuzzy cloud instead of a smooth curtain on either side of her long neck.

At least her dress would have retained its class. The silk linen chemise was mostly printed in a geometric pattern, black, white and sand, with stylish bands of each colour running around the lower half of the skirt. It was very much an adult, career-woman dress, she thought wryly, no shades of the teenager in skimpy beach wear. Life had moved on for her, too.

He broke out of his stillness, his shoulders visibly squaring, chin lifting in a dismissive jerk. "Forgive me for staring. It must be the likeness to Kimberly. The eyes. Same unusual shade of green. It feels…uncanny," he said in an awkward rush.

"I thought she was more like…"

You.

The word teetered on her tongue. She barely bit

it back in time. Her heart somersaulted. Did he know? He wasn't supposed to know. Meredith had no idea what it would mean to his life if he did. She quickly shook her head, dismissing the subject.

"I would have remembered if I'd ever met you," he blurted out with emphatic certainty, his gaze skating over her, taking in the line and length of her, each finely drawn feature of her face. His brow puckered over the sense of recognition. "It has to be the eyes," he murmured more to himself than her.

No, it's all of me, Meredith silently cried, fiercely wishing she could say it.

He shot her a smile that dizzied her with its appealing charm. "I have to confess this situation is like none other I've ever been in. I'm not usually so gauche."

"Please...go on and sit down. Make yourself comfortable," she invited, forcing herself to move to the kitchen doorway. Easier to cover the strain of this meeting with social conventions. "Can I get you a drink? I've opened a bottle of white wine if you'd like a glass, but if you'd prefer tea or coffee...?"

He hesitated, then with an air of playing for time, asked, "Will you have some wine with me?"

"Yes." Why not? She wanted time with him, too, however futile and hurtful it might be.

He nodded. "Thank you."

She took the bottle from the refrigerator, glad to

have something to do. His presence had her nerves jangling. What did he want here? Why had he come?

He didn't sit down. He prowled around, glancing over the contents of her bookcases, taking in the twilight view of the ocean beyond Balmoral Beach from the picture windows behind her lounge suite, eyeing the floral arrangements she'd done for herself, matching them against her furnishings. She'd been pleased with their artistic simplicity. Was he impressed? she wondered. What was he gleaning from this detailed observation of her personal environment?

Strange to think she would never have become a florist but for being pregnant so young, having to drop out of school and being shuttled out of sight to her stepmother's sister in Sydney. Ironic how one thing had led to another, the unpaid apprenticeship in her stepaunt's shop giving her the interest and training to develop a talent she had eventually turned into a successful business.

"Do you share this apartment?" Nick Hamilton asked, tense and ill at ease with the question but asking it nonetheless.

"No," she replied. "It's all mine," she added with a touch of pride, knowing that the home she'd created here proved she was a woman of independent means.

She'd taken her time, selecting what she wanted to live with. The deeply cushioned, squashy leather sofa and chairs were cream so she could dress them up with the multicoloured tapestry cushions she'd stitched over many lonely nights. The wood of the bookshelves and desk was a blond ash, as were the sidetables and her small, four-chair dining suite. The carpet was a dusky pink mushroom.

She'd wanted everything soft and light, uplifting and cosy. It suited her. She fiercely told herself whatever he thought didn't matter. He'd dropped out of her life thirteen years ago and had no right to walk back into it and be critical of anything.

She pushed his glass of wine across the kitchen counter which was open to the living area. "Your drink."

"Thank you. You haven't married?" His eyes were sharply curious and calculating as he came toward her to pick up the wine.

The highly personal inquiry niggled Meredith. He'd spoiled her for any other man and she resented the implication she might have had a free ride on a husband's income. "No. I didn't get this place from a man, Mr. Hamilton," she answered tersely. "I've made my own way through a lot of hard work and a bit of luck. Did you achieve whatever you've got through a woman?"

In a way he had, his sister protecting him from even knowing about a responsibility he had incurred. He'd been left free to prosper in his chosen career instead of being saddled with a young wife and baby. Denise Graham had not only ensured he had every chance to succeed, she'd kept his child for him, too.

He looked abashed. "I didn't mean to suggest…"

Resentment over his intrusion in her life now—far too late—brought a surge of impatience with his purpose. "Just why are you checking me out?" she demanded bluntly. "What answers are you looking for?"

He grimaced at her directness. "I guess you could say we're both faced with a highly delicate situation. I'm trying to ascertain what your attitude might be toward a meeting with Kimberly. Whether it would intrude negatively on the life you have now."

Her mind reeled at the incredible import of what he was saying. A meeting with her daughter? She'd barely dared to hope for it some time in the future when Kimberly was old enough to be her own person. How could this be when she was only twelve?

"Your sister will allow it?" Her throat had gone so dry her voice was a raw croak. Her eyes clung to his in a torment of doubt.

"My sister and her husband were killed in a car accident a year ago. Just before Christmas," he stated quietly. "Kimberly has been in my care ever since."

Shock rolled through her in mind-blowing, heart-wrenching waves. Denise and Colin Graham dead. Since before Christmas last year. And all this time she'd been thinking of them, picturing them going about their lives in their family unit, enjoying all she couldn't enjoy with their daughter. A year! Her daughter had been without a mother, without her adoptive parents, for a whole year!

"I was appointed her legal guardian," Nick Hamilton went on, apparently still unaware he was Kimberly's natural father. His gaze seemed to tunnel into her mind as he added, "I didn't know about you. Didn't know there was any contact between you and my sister."

Meredith closed her eyes. She couldn't bear his non-knowledge of her. And death could have sealed those secret, intimate links forever. It made her sick to think of it.

"Only today did I get your address from the solicitor." His voice strained now, strained with all he didn't know and the fear of the unknown. "He didn't want to give it to me. He argued that Denise's death closed the personal connection between the two of you. He advised against my picking it up."

Fear of the consequences...dear God! The roads that had been travelled to this point! And he was afraid of letting her in to their lives!

"Why did you?" she asked faintly, trying to suppress the bitterness of having no legal rights. Even when the adoptive parents were dead, she couldn't make a claim on her own child.

"For Kimberly. She wants..."

Meredith lifted her lashes enough to see his grimace. He didn't like this. Didn't want it. He'd come against the solicitor's advice, against his own better judgment. His chest rose and fell as he expelled a long, ragged sigh.

"She wants...her *real* mother...for Christmas," he finished flatly.

For Christmas.

Only for Christmas.

A limited encounter...just like with her father. Limited...time out of time to cherish...treasure...haunt. The pain of the limitation sucked the blood from her brain. She clutched at the kitchen counter but couldn't summon the strength to hold on as she slid into dark oblivion.

CHAPTER THREE

NICK picked her up from the kitchen floor and cradled her against his chest. A pins and needles sensation attacked his whole body. It wasn't the effort of carrying her weight. She was not a big woman despite her above-average height. It was the way she seemed to nestle in his arms, her head dropping onto his shoulder as though it belonged there, her long hair flowing across his throat, skeins of silk somehow entangling him with feelings his brain couldn't compute at all. They didn't make sense. At least...not a sense he was ready to acknowledge.

It was too crazy...too beyond rational explanation. He hadn't met her before. He knew he hadn't. Her eyes being the same as Kimberly's was not the answer, either. Kimberly was a child. Meredith Palmer was a woman. How did a woman he didn't know get to walk through his dreams? And to have her materialise in front of him...real flesh and blood...every line of her hauntingly familiar to him... Nick was hopelessly distracted from establishing what he'd come here to do.

He should have approached the salient facts more obliquely, been more sensitive to their impact on her. It was obvious she'd been stressed at not receiving the packet from Denise and his appearance on the scene must have agitated her further despite the reassurance he'd tried to give. Here she was in a dead faint, all because he'd responded without giving enough thought to how it would affect her, and he was still caught up in how she affected him!

Instead of standing in her kitchen like a dumb ox, holding her in his own personal daze, he should be doing something constructive about bringing her back to consciousness. He forced his mind to focus on practicalities.

The sofa in her living room was only a two-seater, not large enough to lay her out comfortably. Bedroom and bathroom had to be nearby. A door stood slightly ajar near one of the bookcases. He carried her to it and manoeuvred her into what proved to be her bedroom.

She was beginning to stir as he lowered her onto the bed, her head rolling restlessly, as though in blind search of something lost. A low moan of longing or some deep inner torment issued from her throat and tugged at his heart. He grasped her hand, his fingers curling tightly around hers, pressing his warmth and strength, wanting to impart she was not alone.

Thinking he should probably get her a glass of water, he glanced around, looking for a door into an ensuite bathroom. And shock hit him again.

The walls were covered with photographs of Kimberly!

Montages of each year of his niece's life hung in frames, interspersed with blow-ups of what were particularly good shots of her, capturing a highly expressive look that seemed to bring her personality stunningly, vibrantly alive in this room.

It was eerie, seeing Kimberly in such close focus from babyhood onward. Nick had seen most of the photographs before at various times, but never in this kind of concentration. The collection, so over-whelmingly displayed, suddenly seemed to smack of unhealthy obsessiveness.

Kimberly's plea...*if my real mother wants me*...became an absurd understatement in the face of so much visual evidence of *wanting*. Nick's head buzzed with a confusion of moral and legal rights. Kimberly was family to him, yet how much more was she to this woman who had given her birth? What if Kimberly's desire to meet her was capricious? What was he setting in motion here?

The warning given by Hector Burnside, Denise's old solicitor, started ringing in Nick's ears. *Leave well enough alone. You don't know what you might be walking into. It could be dangerous ground.*

Maybe he should have heeded the advice of a man who had seen all sides of human nature in his line of work. Nick shook his head over the dilemma he now found himself in. He'd promised Kimberly

an answer from her real mother. In choosing to follow that course, he wasn't sure if he'd stepped into
a dream or a nightmare. Either way, it was too late
to walk out of it.

CHAPTER FOUR

HE WAS holding her hand.

The physical link generated a flood of warm feeling that drove away the chilling fear of the unknown and soothed the whirling chaos in her mind. She hadn't died and moved on to where impossible things were possible. She wasn't dreaming. Nick Hamilton's hand pressed solid substance in a world that had shifted too fast for Meredith to retain a grip on it herself.

The initial confusion of finding herself on her bed, with him sitting beside her, quickly cleared as she remembered what had gone before. "I must have fainted," she croaked in surprise.

Her voice startled him out of the private reverie he'd fallen into. His head jerked around to face her. His eyes had a dazed look. "Yes," he said, his focus sharpening. "You still look pale. Would you like a drink of water?"

She started to prop herself up on her elbow. The room reeled. She fell back on the pillows, hopelessly dizzy. "Yes, please. It might help." She closed her eyes, fighting a wave of nausea. "Sorry…"

"My fault." His weight shifted off the bed. "Be right back."

A combination of shock with too much wine on an empty stomach, Meredith reasoned, wishing she'd had the sense to eat properly. She didn't want Nick Hamilton thinking she was sickly and unable to cope with difficult situations. He might think better of her meeting Kimberly for even a short time.

The longing to see her daughter in the flesh rose so strongly, it overrode every other consideration. To actually see her, watch her in action, listen to her, hear how she felt about so many things…it would be worth any amount of heartache.

Fearing that the opening Nick Hamilton had offered might be withdrawn if his impression of her was negative, Meredith swung her legs off the bed and bent her head down to her knees, determined on regaining her equilibrium. By the time he returned with a glass of water, she had steadied enough to drink it.

The weight of liquid helped settle her stomach. As she put the emptied glass on the bedside table, she glanced up to thank him, only to find he wasn't watching her. He was staring at the photographs on the wall and the grim set to his face did not reflect any pleasure in them.

Her heart sank as she realised what an overwhelming effect the display might have on someone who hadn't seen it, who didn't live with it. She didn't expect others to understand her need for these all too few windows on the life of her lost child and she instinctively recoiled from having that deeply driven maternal need exposed.

"I didn't invite you in here. I don't invite anyone in here," she burst out defensively.

The look he turned on her was so wary it made Meredith feel frantic. Was he in retreat from her? She made a floundering gesture at the photographs.

"I mean all this...it's private," she cried, desperate to win a sympathetic hearing. "You probably take Kimberly and everything about her for granted, having her around you all the time. This is the only way I have of seeing my child grow up."

He shook his head, an appalled expression in his eyes, as though, until this moment, he hadn't begun to comprehend the immense loss she'd borne since Kimberly's birth.

"I gave her up because I thought it best for her. That doesn't mean I love her any less," Meredith asserted with vehement passion, trying to appeal to his sense of fairness.

"I'm sorry," he said gruffly. "I had no idea...no appreciation of..." He gestured apologetically. "I beg your pardon for not being more...prepared."

The father of her child, appearing out of nowhere to suddenly hold out the chance of a reunion—more of a reunion than he knew—how could he have any idea what it meant to her? She ached all over just looking at him, having him near, bringing back the memories of her double grief.

He backed off a step, his face creased in pained concern. "I didn't mean to invade your privacy by bringing you in here. It was only to help. If you'd prefer to recover alone now..."

Anxiety sank its claws in. Was he seizing an opportunity to escape from a situation he was finding too fraught with emotion? Had she just ruined the one chance she might ever have of meeting her daughter? The last thing she wanted was to drive him away. So much was hanging in the balance. She sought frantically for ways to plead her cause and all she could come up with was to beg a stay of judgment.

"Please don't go. I won't collapse on you again."

An aeon seemed to pass as his eyes bored into hers, searching, sifting, undecided as to what was right or wrong. His tension made hers worse. Every nerve in her body was strung tight, willing him to stay and talk until a more favourable position was reached.

"I'll wait in the living room," he said, clearly discomforted by the walls of photographs, the stark evidence of deprived motherhood and the overcharged atmosphere that had risen from its confrontation.

An intense wash of relief brought a hot flow of blood to Meredith's cheeks. Hopefully it gave them a healthy-looking flush. "I'll come with you," she rushed out, afraid to let him out of her sight in case he had second thoughts. "It's food I need. Once I've had something solid to eat I'm sure I'll feel much better."

She quickly pushed up from the bed, swaying slightly before finding her balance. He was beside her in an instant, ready to lend his support. Her eyes pleaded for belief as she assured him, "I'm not usually fragile."

"Take my arm." It was a firm command. "I'll see you seated on your sofa. Then you can tell me what to do in your kitchen to assemble a meal for you."

"I can manage," she protested, intent on proving it.

"So can I," he insisted, intent on taking control.

The need to show independent strength suddenly lost its importance. If she kept him busy with her now, she gained the time to impress him as a responsible person whom he could trust to act both sensibly and sensitively when it came to a meeting with Kimberly. It had to come to that. Had to.

She hooked her arm around his and felt his muscles harden as her hand slid over them. It made her feel skittish, uncertain if he was inwardly recoiling from her touch or reacting to it in the way he once had. Though it was madness to think of that now when so much else was at stake. Besides, the quickly sparked desires of youth hardly fitted into this picture.

Nevertheless, she couldn't help being extremely

aware of him as he matched his steps to hers in their walk to the living room. Her upper arm was tucked against the warm wall of his chest and their hips and thighs brushed, arousing little shivers of sensitivity that sharply reminded her of how intimate they had once been.

Breathing in his aftershave lotion—surely the same tangy scent he'd used then—tickled her nostrils, evoking the memory of how he'd brought all her senses incredibly alive that summer. Every smell had seemed exotic, every colour brighter,, every sound magnified, every taste heightened, every touch…Meredith fiercely clamped down on that line of thought. It was stirring feelings she couldn't afford.

It was a relief when Nick Hamilton deposited her on the sofa and dropped all physical contact with her. He took off so briskly for the kitchen, Meredith suspected it was a relief for him to have some distance between them, too, though his reasons were undoubtedly different. Getting on with the business he'd come about would be very much on his mind.

She watched him taking inventory of the contents of her refrigerator and called, "A sandwich will do. There's bread in the fridge."

Decisive and efficient in his movements, he set out a loaf of bread, butter, a packet of sliced cheese and tomatoes, then switched on the griller at the top of the stove. He was certainly kitchen trained,

Meredith thought, and wondered how much he fended for himself. Was he married?

However pertinent the question was in the circumstances, Meredith shied away from it, reluctant to picture him with a wife. Then she remembered the misery of trying to get along with her stepmother and wondered if Kimberly was suffering the same problem, having lost the parents who had brought her up and then been landed on a woman who had no deep caring for her, a woman who was only there because she was attached to Nick Hamilton.

Meredith knew from first-hand experience how unwanted a girl of Kimberly's age could feel, given such a situation. And it stood to reason that something had to be prompting the desire to meet her real mother. It also stood to reason that a man as attractive as Nick Hamilton would not be without a woman.

Another question sprang to mind. How did Kimberly know about her? Surely it would be uncharacteristic of Denise Graham to reveal anything about Kimberly's *real* mother to the child she was bringing up as her own daughter. It struck Meredith that Nick Hamilton might have more to answer for than he'd like to admit.

"How long has Kimberly known she was adopted?" she asked, feeling the knowledge had to have come after the death of her adoptive parents.

"She found out a week before the car accident that killed Denise and Colin," he answered flatly.

Found out? Dear Heaven! Had the resulting upset contributed to the accident?

Nick Hamilton's dark gaze lifted briefly from the bread he was buttering, a heavy sadness dulling his eyes. "Apparently Denise was sorting through photographs and discussing with Colin which ones to send to you. Kimberly overheard them and pieced the information together." He frowned. "She has a bad habit of eavesdropping. Perhaps being an only child...no sibling to talk to..."

"Did she confront them with it?" Meredith broke in anxiously, imagining the guilt her daughter might feel if there'd been arguments.

He shook his head. "She wanted to think about it. Work out what it meant to her."

A lot of inner turmoil there, Meredith thought, though it was a relief to learn there had been no open conflict for which Kimberly might blame herself.

"Then her world came crashing down," Nick Hamilton continued, "and there were so many changes for her to take on, I guess she clung to what was safely familiar rather than pursue what probably seemed like an intangible dream."

"So *you* didn't talk to her about it?"

"I thought it better not to. She had enough trauma losing one set of parents, let alone two." He grimaced. "She kept it to herself until a few days ago."

Holding such a big secret all that time...holding it in reserve, Meredith thought, and wondered how often her daughter might have fantasised about another life as she tried living with the man who had been legally appointed her guardian, a man who was only an uncle by adoption. Or did Kimberly instinctively feel more closely bonded to him...her *real* father?

Was there an innate tie of blood, whether it was known or not? Would her daughter feel she was a total stranger or would there be an instant, intuitive link between them? The need to know pounded through Meredith, bringing a wave of excitement, of almost unbearable anticipation. It was difficult to contain it but she sternly told herself she had to while a meeting was still not settled.

She watched the only man she had ever loved place the sandwiches he was intent on toasting under the griller and tried to imagine what he was feeling about Kimberly's request, coming virtually out of nowhere. He would not have been *prepared* for that, either. But Nick Hamilton was no dodger of delicate issues. He faced them and dealt with them according to his sense of rightness. It was that very quality of character Meredith had implicitly believed in when she had found herself pregnant.

"You think a rich college boy is going to stand by you?" her stepmother had mocked. "He skipped out fast enough when I told him your age. A guy like that doesn't want to be shackled to a sixteen-year-old country girl who was no more than a Christmas vacation fling to him.''

He hadn't *skipped out*. Meredith hadn't thought it then and she didn't think it now.

It had shocked him when her stepmother had confronted him with how young she was. Meredith had let him assume she was older, knowing she could easily pass for nineteen and desperately wanting to go with him wherever he wanted to take her. She'd argued to herself that love had nothing to do with age.

But Nick had faced the issues squarely and laid them out to her. She still had two more years of school plus tertiary education after that, if she wanted it. There was so much more for her to do and experience and think about before tying herself to anyone or anything. She should be free to make the choices that would best suit her. The love they felt for each other could be recaptured when she was older. He didn't feel right about taking up her life while she still had so much in front of her.

He had given her his address and suggested they send each other Christmas cards if they both wanted to keep the connection going. No commitment. But there was no harm in maintaining a friendly communication once a year. When she was twenty-one...

"Isn't eighteen old enough?" she'd protested,

devastated at the thought of waiting so many years before they could be lovers again.

"It wouldn't be fair," he'd answered ruefully. "Any more than it would be fair of me to stay on here, Merry. The more deeply we get involved the harder it will be to part."

He'd gone that very day, the day after her stepmother had discovered them making love on the back veranda and created such an ugly scene, accusing Nick of taking advantage of a girl who was barely past being a minor. Despite his shock, Nick hadn't allowed her stepmother to turn what had been beautiful into something low and dirty. And though he had left her, it wasn't without the promise of a future for them…if their love held true. Giving her his address was proof of his good faith. He wouldn't have done that if he was *skipping out* on her.

Meredith had known her pregnancy would come as another shock to him. He'd taken precautions every time they'd made love. How they'd failed she didn't know but she'd had no doubt Nick would stand by her. He was kind and caring and responsible and honourable. She couldn't imagine him letting her down.

It hurt, even now, thinking back to the Christmas after the birth of their baby. Secretly, she'd been so sure a Christmas card would come from him. Even though he was overseas in America, he would think of her and write and then she'd have a contact address and be able to write back, telling him what had happened. She had dreamed of him flying home and reclaiming their child from his sister. They'd be married and…but no Christmas card had come from him.

The only communication had been the first promised packet of photographs from his sister.

So had begun the painful process of accepting that Denise Graham had told the truth about his losing all memory of the time they'd spent together. Or that Nick had put her out of his life. Either way, it was too late to change her mind about giving up her baby daughter. That decision was irrevocable.

But some dreams refused to die. A year later she'd succumbed to the temptation of going to the address Nick had given her, the Grahams' address, hoping to see him since his two years in the U.S. were up, wanting the chance to know for certain how matters stood between them. The Grahams had moved. None of their neighbours knew where they'd gone. The one avenue she'd had to him was closed.

She'd told herself to get on with her life, and she had, but for a long, long time the dream had persisted that he would turn up one day and make everything right again. And here he was, but with no memory of her, and trying to make things right for the child he thought of as his niece.

He emerged from the kitchen, carrying a plate of toasted sandwiches, and Meredith steeled herself to keep a calm composure, determined on convincing him she would do what was best for Kimberly, the welfare and happiness of her daughter being her first consideration. But she couldn't stop her eyes from wandering over him, nor could she quell the wish for some sign of the love they had once shared.

Her pulse quickened with each step he took toward her. As he bent to set the plate on the coffee table in front of her, her eyes feasted on his face, admiring the long thick sweep of his eyelashes—their daughter had inherited them—and retracing the sensual contours of his mouth, remembering the explosive passion of his kisses. Her muscles clenched, wanting the release he had once given them, and Meredith savagely berated herself for being unable to suppress the desires he stirred.

"Are you married?" she asked, driven to know if he was out of bounds to her. If he was, maybe she could put this intense distraction aside and concentrate solely on establishing time with Kimberly.

"No." He flashed a sharp look at her before moving to settle in the armchair on the other side of the table.

Meredith struggled to maintain a natural air of inquiry. That one brief word eased the terrible tightness in her chest. It was like a song of hope in her ears. For a moment or two her mind danced with wonderful possibilities. Then the realities of today's world crashed in, reminding her of the common-place arrangements that didn't require marriage.

"Do you live with...with a partner?" She couldn't bring herself to say *lover*.

"No." He sat facing her, watching her, and Meredith could only hope he couldn't see she was giddy with relief. His expression was carefully schooled to give nothing of his thoughts away as he slowly added, "I employ a woman to come in weekdays and be there after school hours. She also looks after Kimberly whenever I'm out in the evening. She's with her now. They get on quite well."

He was assuring her his guardianship was not at fault. A smile burst across her face. "That's good," she said, wildly understating what she really felt.

He stared at her so long the smile stiffened and faded as self-consciousness swept in, along with the worry she had overstepped some line he'd drawn in his mind.

"Eat," he commanded.

She quickly pounced on a toasted triangle, glad to have something to do until he showed more of his hand. Never had she enjoyed the taste of melted cheese on tomato so much. It was as though her whole body zinged with a new appreciation of life and a greed for all it could offer.

Nick Hamilton was with her again.

He had their daughter in his safekeeping.

And he wasn't tied to any other woman.

CHAPTER FIVE

NICK couldn't get her smile out of his head, her face lighting up like a Christmas tree, jolting him anew with the sense of recognition. He didn't believe in all that New Age stuff about having known each other in previous lives. He had no answer for what he was feeling and it was bugging the hell out of him. Even the touch of her made him jangle with the tension of hormones running riot, body chemistry leaping out of control.

He watched her eat the toasted sandwiches he'd made, brooding over why this woman—this stranger—should affect him so strongly. On the surface she was no more attractive than Rachel. In strictly physical terms, she was slimmer, not as curvy, not as pretty. Yet more striking, more…electric somehow.

He was finding this encounter so damned disturbing he wished it was at an end. In fact, there was no reason to prolong it since there seemed to be no serious impediment to the meeting with Kimberly.

Only God knew where that would end. It was impossible for him to judge.

All he knew was Kimberly was not about to let it rest until it happened and he didn't feel right about keeping them apart. Let the pieces fall however they would, he thought, glumly acknowledging that the outcome would most probably be out of his control, as well.

"Would lunch this Saturday suit you?" he asked.

Another smile. It had the kick of a mule.

"Any day at all. Any time," she answered eagerly.

He frowned. It sounded too carefree. "Don't you work?"

"I run my own business. I can arrange my time as I like," came the ready reply. A touch of pride, as well.

"What do you do?" Kimberly would want to know and his own curiosity was piqued.

"I have contracts with hotels and restaurants to supply their floral arrangements. My company name is *Flower Power.*"

Impressive. He glanced at the clever piece of floral art on the coffee table. He'd admired it earlier...just three perfect blooms at different heights set in an interesting variety of leaves...very simple yet very pleasing to the eye. "Your work?"

"Yes. Do you like it?"

He nodded. "A fine dramatic touch. Did you study art?"

She looked pleased. "No. All hands-on experience."

"Probably the best teacher anyway," he conceded, warming to her warmth. "Though you must have an innate talent for it."

"I enjoy the work." Her mesmerisingly familiar green eyes sparkled with delight. "Flowers give so much pleasure and they can light up a room."

You can, too, he thought, wondering if there was a man in her life. She didn't have a husband or a live-in lover but that didn't mean she wasn't attached to someone. As he was, to Rachel. To Nick's further confusion, something in him strongly wanted to reject both their involvements with other people, no matter how well-founded they were. Again, the irrational nature of the feeling prompted him to finish up here as fast as he could.

She'd eaten the sandwiches and appeared to have fully recovered from the faint. He could leave with an easy conscience. "Do you know the Harbour Restaurant underneath the opera house?"

"Yes."

They could sit out on the open deck under an umbrella, he decided. The pleasant venue with the wide view of the harbour and the passing parade of people should provide a relaxed atmosphere, if anything about this first mother-daughter meeting could be relaxed.

"I'll book a table for twelve o'clock." He stood

up, softening his leave-taking with a rueful smile. "I doubt Kimberly will be able to wait to a later time. And I mustn't keep her waiting any longer now. She won't go to bed until I return with news of you."

"Of course. I hope…" She flushed as she rose quickly from the sofa to see him out. Her eyes filled with an eloquent appeal that tunneled straight into his gut. "Please tell her I'm looking forward enormously to our meeting."

Compassion forced him to a kindly warning. "Don't bank too much on it, Miss Palmer. Kimberly's a good kid at heart but she's a bit mixed up about future direction at the moment. She'll be starting high school next year and choosing what school has become an issue. You seem to have become part of that issue. She *is* only twelve. I don't think she comprehends…the larger picture."

Meredith Palmer drew a deep breath and sighed in wry resignation. "Whatever happens, at least I'll have a little while with her. Thank you for allowing it, Mr. Hamilton. I'm very grateful to you."

Any crumb from the table was better than nothing.

That depressing thought stayed with him as he drove away. It was wrong for so little to mean so much. The walls of photographs in her bedroom kept flashing through his mind. He'd never given any consideration to the effect on a woman who gave up her baby for adoption. It had to be trau-matic...a wound that never healed.

He wondered what forces had played a part in Meredith Palmer's decision, whether she'd been in her right mind at the time or pressured beyond bear-ing into a sacrifice she had regretted ever since. Had her family been straitlaced, shamed by their daugh-ter falling pregnant, denying her the chance of keeping her baby by withholding support?

She must have been very young. It was difficult to tell a woman's age but Meredith Palmer looked to be only in her twenties now. At fourteen or fif-teen, possibly suffering post-natal depression, a baby must have seemed an overwhelming respon-sibility, the problem of coping properly with it in-surmountable if her family wasn't prepared to help.

I gave her up because I thought it best for her.

Such sad, hopeless words.

He should have asked what connection there'd been to his sister for the private adoption to be ar-ranged. He must remember to do that. He wanted to know.

Until Kimberly had told him about the photo-graphs and he'd subsequently tackled Denise's old solicitor about them, he had assumed the adoption had taken place through normal channels. Denise and Colin had talked often of having applied to the government agency. Their names had been on a waiting list. When they'd written to him in the

States to tell him of their new baby he had simply thought the wait had ended. They had not enlightened him otherwise.

Why the secret?

Why the photographs?

Some kind of guilt on his sister's part?

In the face of Meredith Palmer's yearning for her child, he felt guilty himself for having her in his keeping. Yet Kimberly was his family and had been all her life. He'd always had a soft spot for her. He strongly recoiled from the idea of giving her up...even to go to her real mother.

Perhaps a sharing arrangement could be made.

That, of course, would depend on how the meeting turned out. At this point he couldn't predict how Kimberly would react to it. He didn't know what she was secretly expecting or wanting, beyond satisfying the need to see.

She fell upon him the moment he entered his apartment. "What's she like? Is she pretty? Does she want to see me? Did you set up a meeting?"

"Yes to the last three questions. Now please hold on a moment!" he commanded, pulling her hyperactive body back off him and setting her a pace away.

She radiated excitement, hands waving like a baby, ponytail swinging, her face aglow with wildly impatient anticipation, her glittering green eyes—Meredith Palmer's eyes—stabbing into him, desperately eager for information. "Don't be a stodge, Uncle Nick! I'm dying to know all about her."

"Let me pay Mrs. Armstrong first, Kimberly." He turned to the woman who was packing up her knitting, ready to leave. "Any calls, Fran?"

"Only the one, from Rachel Pearce. She asked if you'd return it tonight at your convenience." Having gathered up her belongings, she headed toward them and the front door, a smile of caring concern sweeping them both. "I do hope this business with Kimberly's mother turns out well. It doesn't always, you know. I've read so many stories in magazines..."

"I guess life is about taking chances, Fran," Nick cut in, his smile appealing for no negative comment. It served no good purpose at this point.

She nodded, an obliging soul, always prepared to ride along with what he wanted. A widow in her fifties, her children had grown up and flown the home nest, leaving her with no role to play until they gave her grandchildren. Her hair was unashamedly grey, permed tightly for tidiness, her face and figure pleasantly plump, her clothes matronly, and she knitted soft toys interminably. She dearly wanted to be a doting grandmother. Looking after Kimberly helped to fill that hole in her life and Nick was grateful she was so good at it.

He added a tip to the usual fee.

"You are a good man," she said warmly. "I'll

see you tomorrow, Kimberly. Don't be dancing around all night, there's a dear girl. You need your sleep.''

"Good night, Mrs. Armstrong. Thanks for being here. I'll settle down after I dig everything out of Uncle Nick," Kimberly promised breezily.

Dig was the operative word. She attacked again the moment the door closed behind her minder, bubbling around him with avid curiosity. Feeling in need of a stiff drink, Nick moved across the dining area to the liquor cabinet as he answered the first burst of questions, trying to give the detail Kimberly demanded. He opened a bottle of port and poured a generous measure into a glass. The fortified liquor seemed highly appropriate for these circumstances.

He carried it over to the lounge, finding himself sweeping a critical gaze over the furnishings he'd lived with for years; black leather upholstery on both dining and lounge suites, glass tables, blue-grey carpet, black fixtures for the television and hi-fi system, a few sculptured pieces he'd fancied, some provocative modern paintings he didn't really look at anymore.

He'd liked her living room. More warmth. More individual, personal touches like the colourful, hand-stitched cushions and the flowers and the books...the sense of it all being an integral part of her. Then the intensely private, secret life in the bedroom revealing the deeper side of her, not shown to anyone. He shouldn't have seen it, but he had, and now he couldn't forget it.

He sank onto one of the sofas and made himself comfortable for the important task of instructing his niece on what would be acceptable behaviour with her *real* mother. Kimberly sprawled on the sofa opposite his and kept prodding and prying, extracting all the information he was prepared to give on Meredith Palmer, then fell into musing on what she should wear on Saturday, keen to make a positive impression on the woman who had given her birth. Nick mentally girded his loins and plunged in to the more sensitive aspect of the meeting.

"I appreciate you find this very exciting, Kimberly," he said quietly, "but you must understand it is strictly a getting-to-know-you meeting on Saturday. Don't turn it into a battleground, playing Miss Palmer against me..."

"I wouldn't do that, Uncle Nick," she cried earnestly.

"...Or against Rachel."

She flushed, her eyes wavering from his.

"You'll be meeting a person with highly sensitive feelings about having given up her child," he went on gravely. "It would be wrong to embroil her in an argument about a school. Don't make her feel you're using her, Kimberly."

Discomfort on that point clearly showed as she

plucked at one of the blue decorator cushions on the sofa. Then her gaze flashed up in belligerent challenge. "Wouldn't she care how I feel about it?"

"Yes. She'd care. And you would make her feel unhappy and helpless because she has no say in it. She lost her right to have any say in your life when she agreed to your adoption."

"But that's not fair!" she burst out. "She's my real mother."

"Do you want to know her...or do you want to use her, Kimberly?" he bored in.

She gestured an agitated protest. "Of course I want to *know* her..."

But she had been nursing other items on her agenda.

Nick followed up relentlessly. "I would hope you wouldn't be so petty or so mean and selfish as to complain about your personal problems when meeting you is the fulfilment of a dream to her."

"A dream?"

"She had the photographs to build a dream of you, Kimberly. I'd like her to feel proud of the person you are now. If nothing else, you owe it to the mother who loved and cared for you since you were a baby to show she did a good job of bringing you up."

Her face puckered. "Mum wouldn't mind me meeting her, would she, Uncle Nick? I mean, she did send the photographs so she must have wanted her to see how I was growing up.''

"I think this meeting would have her blessing, Kimberly, but I also think she'd like it best if Miss Palmer met you and thought she couldn't have done a better job of teaching you good manners and being nice to people. You know your Mum set a lot of store by that.''

Tears glittered in her eyes. "I'll be good, Uncle Nick.'' She came off her sofa in a rush and landed on his lap, her arms flung around his neck and her head nestling on his shoulder. "I'll make Mum real proud of me. I promise,'' she whispered huskily.

He hugged her and rubbed his cheek over her hair, loving the child she still was and deeply moved by her uninhibited affection. She belonged with him. She was the only family he had left. Yet he knew every time he looked at her now he would be reminded of Meredith Palmer and her enduring love for the child she had given up. He felt caught in a hopeless quandary.

"I think your real mother will think you're wonderful,'' he murmured. "The best Christmas present she's ever had.''

A deep sigh. "I want her to like me.''

"I'm sure she will.'' He dropped a kiss on her temple. "Best off to bed now, Kimberly. Sweet dreams.''

"Good night, Uncle Nick. And thanks for everything.'' She pecked his cheek and was off, pausing at the hall to the bedrooms to say, ''I've dreamed about her, too. My real mother, I mean. Ever since I knew I was adopted I've been dreaming about her.''

She didn't wait for a reply. It was simply confiding the truth to him. Nick was left thinking of his own dreams, wondering how his subconscious had conjured up the image of Meredith Palmer. Perhaps he'd seen a photograph of her. If his sister had known her she might have had a photograph.

But why didn't he remember it? And why of all the women in the photographs his sister had taken over decades, had *she* become a dream-woman to him...a figure that called to him yet remained tantalisingly out of reach.

He'd figured it was symbolic of his disappointment in being unable to strike a soul mate amongst the women he'd met and dated. Symbolic also of a need to believe there was someone still out there for him, and if only he persisted long enough he would find her.

But for the fantasy figure to match up to someone in real life... Nick clenched his teeth. He was not going to consider supernatural stuff. The coincidence had to have a rational explanation. And the effect Meredith Palmer was having on him...that was mixed up with her matching a dream. Naturally, something so unexpected triggered confusion. The power of her impact would be much less when they met again on Saturday.

Determinedly pushing aside her lingering influence on him, Nick pushed up from the sofa and went into the kitchen to call Rachel. It was almost eleven o'clock but he knew Rachel rarely went to bed before midnight. Besides, she'd asked for him to call and talking to her might restore his sanity.

When her voice came over the line, he was vexed to find himself comparing the bright, brisk, matter-of-fact tone to Meredith Palmer's softer lilt. "It's Nick," he said quickly.

"Dear Nick, I'm so glad you got back to me." An injection of warmth that should have lightened his mood, but didn't. "I have an invite to Christmas cocktails on Harvey Sinclair's yacht. Saturday evening. Six o'clock start. Want to partner me?"

Harvey Sinclair was a big fish in the financial world. Rachel was bound to be eager to go. Good contacts would abound at such a party. Normally Nick would have given an automatic yes, but he found himself hesitating, looking for a way out of it.

"I'd rather not," he said honestly. "Can you find someone else to go with?"

A pause, her shrewd mind sifting signals. "Some problem, Nick?"

He sighed over his own unease. "I've set up a meeting between Kimberly and her real mother on

Saturday. I don't know how it will turn out, Rachel.''

"And you want to stick around. Understandable, Nick. Tricky business.''

"Very.'' He appreciated her quick grasp of the situation. He rarely had to explain much to Rachel. It made conversation flow so easily.

"Not to worry,'' she assured him without a trace of feeling put out. "I don't mind going by myself. I intended to circulate anyway. I'll tell you all about it when next we get together.''

"I'll look forward to it.''

"I hope the meeting...well, I hope it helps Kimberly.''

"Thanks for your caring, Rachel. I'm sorry about her attitude toward you. I wish...''

"Hey! She's had a lot on her mind. Maybe she'll give me a break when some of it's been lifted.''

He smiled at her ready good humour. "Well, have a good time Saturday night. I'll see you soon.''

It was a comfortable note on which to end the call, causing Nick to reflect that his relationship with Rachel was comfortable. It was effortlessly companionable, easy, undemanding.

What it lacked was passion.

The thought struck Nick forcefully and stayed with him long after he'd gone to bed. Rachel was always reasonable. So was he. Two eminently reasonable human beings, feeling no great highs but no great lows, either. Safe.

Passion was a roller-coaster, an explosive force, a whirlwind, and he suddenly knew that was what Meredith Palmer represented, what he'd felt caught up in while he was with her...passion in all its range and dimensions.

It was pervasively disturbing.

And intensely alluring.

CHAPTER SIX

MEREDITH strolled slowly along the wide promenade that edged Circular Quay, filling in time since she was far too early for the lunch appointment with Kimberly and Nick Hamilton. If she'd stayed any longer in her apartment she would have undoubtedly changed clothes again, succumbing to the frenzy of anxiety that had forced her into four different outfits, dithering over what would be most appropriate and appealing for this critical meeting with her daughter.

She had tried to think what a twelve-year-old girl might want her mother to look like; smart and classy, soft and feminine, casual and approachable, bright and boldly chic...there were so many looks one might present. She'd swung through the lot; dress, suit, jazzy separates, tailored slacks, jeans. What she had finally chosen was probably too formal but at least she always felt good in it.

The colour suited her—a lemon-yellow floral print on white pique cotton. The short-sleeved, figure-hugging jacket had a wide, white collar with dramatic lapels, setting off her long neck and providing a sharp contrast to the dark blond fall of her hair. The narrow skirt was a trendy length, ending just above her knees. Low-heeled lemon-yellow shoes and a matching handbag added the fashion touch that lifted the outfit into top class. It had invariably drawn compliments.

The plain truth was, Meredith admitted to herself, vanity had won out in the end. She wanted Kimberly to feel proud of her mother. And however foolish it might be, she wanted Nick Hamilton to take a second look at her...a long second look.

Although she knew next to nothing about him now—how his character had developed over the years or what turns his life had taken—the long-cherished memories of their young love had resurfaced, tantalising her with possibilities that kept burrowing into her heart. Some dreams didn't die easily. Not even in the bright light of day.

It couldn't be brighter than it was at the moment, she thought with wry humour. The sparkling waters of the harbour reflected the clear blue of a cloudless summer sky. Sunshine glittered off the tiled roofs of the opera house, accentuating the effect of sails billowed to full stretch. Boats and ferries left a wake of frothy waves, trails of brilliant white bubbles. It was the kind of day that made people feel it was great to be alive.

Happy tourists were out en masse, a river of colour streaming around her. Christmas was everywhere; gaudy and glorious decorations, street-sellers pressing their wares as gifts, Santa Claus greeting children. Buskers provided entertainment, well-loved carols being the obvious favourite. Gaiety and goodwill were in the air and Meredith no longer cared that Kimberly had only asked to see her for Christmas. It was a start...and who knew where it would finish?

She skirted groups posing for photographs against the background of the huge coathanger bridge that spanned the harbour. So many smiling faces. They made her smile, too, lifting her spirits. Anything was possible.

Although Nick Hamilton didn't remember it, today was the anniversary of when they'd first met, thirteen years ago. If he could only see her with the same eyes as then, the magical connection could happen again, couldn't it?

It was still ten minutes short of noon when she arrived at the large apron deck on the harbour side of the opera house, but she wasn't the first to arrive. Despite the milling crowd enjoying the view from this marvellous vantage point, she spotted Nick Hamilton immediately. He was standing in profile, leaning on the railing near where the water taxis drew in to set down or pick up theatregoers.

Meredith instantly halted, needing to catch her breath and give her heart time to recover its normal beat, or at least an approximation of it. Her gaze targeted the girl beside him. She faced the water, her back turned to Meredith, but it had to be Kimberly...her daughter...her baby grown to girlhood.

She was tall for her age, with the supple slenderness of a fast-growing child. Her long legs were encased in lime green jeans which she'd teamed with a white T-shirt patterned with orange and lemon and lime squiggles. A bubbly lemon band circled her black ponytail and she wore lemon sneakers on her feet. White socks.

She obviously liked bright colours. Meredith felt a wave of glad relief that her own colour choice in this instance fitted her daughter's taste.

A movement caught her eye, Nick Hamilton's head turning toward her. She looked back at him, her pulse racing again. He stiffened as his gaze connected with hers. The impact moment of recognition seemed to screech along every nerve in Meredith's body. Did he know her this time? Had she struck some chord in his memory? He stared at her as though she were a mirage he couldn't quite believe in.

Then he visibly shook himself out of the hypnotic fixation and touched Kimberly on the shoulder. His mouth formed words Meredith couldn't hear. The effect on the girl was instant. She swung around, her vibrant face lit with eager anticipation, her eyes swiftly scanning faces, her body tense with excitement.

The tug on Meredith's heart was so strong, her feet started forward, walking fast, faster, the need to close the distance between them urgent. She wanted to sing out, ''I'm here!'' She wanted to sweep her child up and hug her in an ecstasy of loving, in a wild celebration of both of them being alive, being able to touch and feel and know that their coming together was real.

Nick Hamilton's hand lifted, pointing direction. Perhaps he said more. Kimberly's gaze zeroed in on Meredith and stuck, her eyes rounding in stunned surprise, her mouth falling open. She didn't move. It was Nick Hamilton who moved, stepping out as though in warning to Meredith to hold back a little, approach more slowly.

The impulses surging through her wavered as caution caught at them. Sober reason clicked into her mind driving back the wild rush of emotion, insisting that too much too soon was not a wise course in these circumstances. She was a stranger to her child, a stranger who had to win her trust and love.

Tears blurred her eyes as she struggled to contain the tumult of feeling. A smile, she thought. At least she could show her love in a smile. Her legs obeyed her command to come to a halt beside the man who had initiated this meeting and she gave her daughter the brightest smile she could dredge up, knowing it wobbled but trying her utmost to hold it and inject it with all the warmth of a welcome that had been waiting so terribly long.

"Kimberly...this is your mother...Meredith Palmer," came the gentle introduction from Nick Hamilton.

Kimberly closed her mouth and swallowed hard. Her eyes clung to Meredith's face.

"I'm so very happy to meet you, Kimberly," Meredith managed huskily.

"You're beautiful," came the awed whisper.

"You are, too," was the only answer that came to mind. It was true. The combination of her green eyes with Nick's black hair was stunning. She'd inherited their best features in a pleasing amalgamation that was uniquely her own.

"You could say hello, Kimberly," Nick prompted in a kindly, indulgent tone.

She flushed, quickly offering her hand for Meredith to clasp. "Hello," she echoed. "I'm really glad you came. I'm sorry I got so dumb. Uncle Nick said you were pretty, but you could be a model. Honest!"

The awkward, eager words tumbled out artlessly. Meredith's smile threatened to wobble again as she curled her hand around the smaller one of her daughter's, such soft young skin, warm flesh and blood, solid and real. Her mind swirled around the heady sensation of touch. It was hard to drive it into making conversation.

"Not a day has gone by that I haven't thought of you, wondering where you were and how you were doing," she said softly. "It always helped that I knew you had good parents, Kimberly, and I'm sorry you lost them." She couldn't resist squeezing the small hand as she added, "I wish I could have been there for you then."

"It's okay," came the shy reply. "I had Uncle Nick. He's pretty good really."

"That could be the best compliment I've had for some time," Nick drawled in a teasing lilt. "Maybe I should get it in writing. Will you witness it, Miss Palmer?"

It lightened the emotion-charged atmosphere and served as a warning for Meredith to ease off.

"Oh, come on, Uncle Nick!" Kimberly rolled her eyes at him. "I only say you're a stodge when you're being a stick-in-the-mud." She withdrew her hand to gesture a reproof. "We're supposed to be saying good things today."

"I stand corrected," he said with mock ruefulness. "From here on in I'll tell Miss Palmer you're a perfect angel."

Kimberly sighed in exasperation.

Meredith laughed, happy to see the easy rapport between the two, the love that was taken for granted. It was obvious her daughter was fine and Nick was taking good care of her.

Kimberly gave her a look that appealed for understanding. "I'm not a perfect angel..."

"None of us are," Meredith assured her with a grin. "On the other hand, it's such a perfect day, let's enjoy it all we can."

"Starting with food," Nick popped in. "I don't know about you, Miss Palmer, but the nervous energy that's been swirling around me this morning seems to have drained my stomach. I'm starving."

He was handling this so well. No constraint. Smoothing the path. Her eyes thanked him, loving him for caring to make it as right as he could. "Lunch would be good," she agreed, half turning and holding out her left hand for Kimberly to take if she wanted to, smiling encouragement.

She took it. "Uncle Nick said this restaurant served super food. I hope you'll like it." Eager to impress.

"How could I not? It has such a lovely position." *And I've got the best company in the world.* Her heart was so full it was difficult not to pour out her feelings. Only the thought of overwhelming the child stopped her. She forced herself to hold her hand lightly as they walked along together, chatting about food preferences.

Long tubs of shrubs formed a demarcation line between the outside dining area of the restaurant and the public domain. A waiter took Nick's name and ushered them to a table by the water. A wide umbrella overhead provided welcome shade, lowering the glare and protecting them from the harmful rays of the sun.

They had an unrestricted view of Fort Denison, the small island in the harbour where the worst criminals were marooned in the early convict days. *Pinchgut,* it had been commonly called, because the men had been left for lengthy periods with only very small rations. Like her with Kimberly, Meredith thought, remembering the long emptiness in between the once-a-year photographs and the subsequent craving for more.

She watched her daughter covertly as they settled into their chairs, secretly feasting on the wealth of detail that photographs could never impart; the way she moved, the wonderful mobility of her face as her expressions changed, the bright intelligence in her eyes, the fascinating dimple in one cheek, the holding-her-own tilt of her chin as she bantered with the man she believed was her uncle.

A jug of ice water was quickly brought, menus handed around. The business of selecting their orders helped to set a more relaxed mood, though Meredith noticed Kimberly took every discreet opportunity to eye her in more lingering detail. Meredith fiercely hoped she liked all she saw.

The menu was a blur of choices. It didn't matter what she ate. It was highly doubtful she'd even taste it. When the waiter returned, Kimberly ordered battered fish fillets and chips and Meredith said she'd have the same. Nick decided on a chicken dish and added a green salad for three as an accompaniment to their meal. He asked if she'd like to share a bottle of wine but Meredith declined, not wanting her perceptions even slightly fuzzied. They all requested soft drinks.

"Uncle Nick said you live at Balmoral. Do you like the beach?" Kimberly asked.

"Very much. I was brought up in Coff's Harbour on the far north coast." She flicked a glance at the man who had met and known her there. His expression held speculative interest, no personal reaction to the name of the seaside town. "The beach used to be my playground," she added to Kimberly. "Since I came to Sydney I've always lived somewhere near one."

"Because it reminds you of home?"

No, not home, Meredith thought, shaking her head. Her stepmother had never really provided a *home*. "More because it offers so many free pleasures," she answered. "Walking along the shore, breathing in the fresh sea air, surfing. What about you? Do you enjoy swimming?"

"Mmmh." Pride in her achievement danced in her eyes. "I'm fairly good at it actually."

"School champion for her age this year," Nick said dryly. "She's a regular mermaid."

Kimberly laughed, bubbling over with pleasure.

"Uncle Nick's going to teach me windsurfing over the summer holidays."

"That sounds wonderful," Meredith enthused, her heart turning over as her mind suddenly filled with the memory of learning the same skills from him thirteen summers ago; catching the wind, skimming over the water, riding the waves, the exhilaration of it made even more intoxicating because he was watching, sharing, enjoying it with her.

The ache for what she had had and lost welled up in her. She was glad Kimberly had such a good relationship with her father, but seeing it, experiencing it, made the hurt of being shut out of their lives all these years so much worse. What she had missed...and could never have...because the time that could have been spent together was gone and the memories belonged to them, not to her.

"Miss...Miss Palmer?" Kimberly called hesitantly.

Miss Palmer...a stranger.

Meredith had automatically veiled her thoughts and it was an effort to lift her lashes and summon a smile. "Yes?"

Kimberly searched her eyes worriedly. "You were looking so sad. Did I say something wrong?"

"No." Meredith's smile turned wry. "It's just...I wish I could have been there to cheer you on when you won the swimming championship."

"Mum always used to come and watch me."

Mum... It was like a stab to the heart. But Denise Graham wouldn't be there to watch her adopted daughter windsurfing. The past was gone and Meredith silently berated herself for brooding over it. She had to concentrate on the future.

"I'm sure she was very proud of you," she said as warmly as she could.

Kimberly shifted uncomfortably. "It's sort of weird. I know you're my real mother...but Mum was Mum...and you look so young..."

"Are you worried about what to call me?" Meredith put in helpfully.

It triggered an instant appeal. "Uncle Nick said maybe your first name...if that was okay by you. It feels a bit stodgy, calling you Miss Palmer."

"Try Merry." The special name slipped out before Meredith thought better of it.

"Merry...short for Meredith," Kimberly mused. "Is that what your friends call you?"

She hesitated, glancing quickly at Nick Hamilton. He looked back at her quizzically. The name had no relevance to him. Somehow that painful truth goaded her to say to their daughter, "Only one other person has ever used that name for me."

"Your mother?" came the quick guess.

"No."

"Who then?" Curiosity piqued.

There was almost a savage, primitive satisfaction in relating how it had been, knowing that Nick

Hamilton was listening, unaware she was speaking of him. "It was your father, Kimberly. Your real father. When he met me he said it was like all the Christmas lights in the world switching on inside him and when he asked me my name and I told him, he shook his head and said…"

Suddenly she choked, the memory so vivid, and here she was, all these years later, sitting with the heart-wrenching outcome of the one love affair of her life…with a daughter she didn't know and the lover who didn't know her.

"What did he say?" Kimberly prompted avidly, caught up in the story about her real father, her eyes begging to be told.

She had to go on. Impossible to retract or retreat. Meredith was intensely conscious of Nick Hamilton listening…sitting very still and listening as she forced the words past the lump in her throat.

"He said…not Meredith. Merry. It has to be Merry. I laughed and asked him why…"

"Yes?" Kimberly urged.

Meredith took a deep breath to steady her voice. "It was Christmas time, you see. Just as it is now. And he looked at me, his eyes sparkling so much it felt like I was in a shower of beautiful fireworks. I've never forgotten the moment or the reply he gave me."

She paused, fighting back tears.

Kimberly was breathlessly hanging on hearing it all.

Nick Hamilton remained still and silent.

"Merry..." she repeated softly, hugging the poignant memory to herself as she turned her head away from both of them and stared out across the endlessly shifting waters to the old stone fort that had once served as a prison. History, she thought. It's past history. Old history. Forgotten history. Only she remembered the words. She could still hear them, just as they had been spoken, and the long echo of happy pleasure furred her voice as she added, "...*Because you're my Merry Christmas.*"

CHAPTER SEVEN

LIKE all the Christmas lights in the world switching on inside him...

Nick found himself captivated by that image, realising it was uncannily accurate. He sat staring at the woman who'd conjured it up, wishing he could read her mind, wishing she was not such a disturbing enigma to him.

He hadn't even tried to define what he felt when he'd spotted her amongst the crowd. She'd been standing still, her whole being concentrated on him, an energy force that zapped across the distance between them and set off a host of electric charges through his nervous system. The impact had stunned him for several seconds.

She was still affecting him. Not only was the physical attraction disconcertingly strong, his mind was being continually teased by the sense of recognition. He figured the only way to deal with that was to wait for her to reveal more about herself, hopefully something that would explain the inexplicable to him.

Whoever Kimberly's real father was, he'd undoubtedly been a smooth-tongued bastard to come up with that apt and evocative description. It was all too clear that lover boy had taken his *Merry Christmas* and left her pregnant, the fanciful words just so much tinsel when it came to a test of integrity and commitment.

Looking at the sad wistfulness on her face, the memory of him lingering in her mind, Nick had no trouble believing she'd fallen for the guy like a ton of bricks. Then the harsh realities of being left with a baby must have fallen on her like a ton of bricks.

She couldn't have been much more than a kid; innocent, naive, trusting, caught up in romantic excitement, falling in love for probably the first time. The odd part was, she didn't sound bitter about the lover who hadn't stood by her. It was almost as though she cherished the memory.

Kimberly heaved a huge, sentimental sigh over the romantic story. "I think that's lovely," she softly gushed. "Thank you for telling me, Merry."

Her mother's face lightened as she swung her attention back to his niece...her daughter. "It was the best Christmas of my life until now. Meeting you today is the most wonderful thing that's happened to me since."

"But you must have had good times in between." Kimberly was appalled at the idea of twelve Christmases going by with not much to say for them. They had always been a big deal for her.

"Don't you have a family to go to?" she asked in concern.

A sad shake of the head. "My mother died when I was eight. My father remarried when I was twelve. He was swept off rocks by a big wave while fishing and drowned when I was fourteen." She grimaced. "Which left me with my stepmother."

"You didn't like her?" Kimberly popped in.

"We didn't get on very well." The reply was clearly understated.

Kimberly flashed a pointed look at Nick. The message was loud and clear. She didn't want a stepmother. If he was thinking of marrying Rachel he'd better take notice.

Rachel, however, had never been further from Nick's mind and the idea of marrying her had slipped into limbo. His thoughts were constantly revolving around the woman sitting opposite him.

Having shot him her warning, Kimberly persisted on the subject with her *real* mother. "I bet she didn't want you with her."

"You're right," came the ready concession. "She made me feel like leftover baggage from her marriage to my father. The last straw for her was my getting pregnant at sixteen. She called me a lot of nasty names but none of them was true." Her expression softened. "I loved your father, Kimberly. He was the only one."

The warm feeling in her voice curled around

Nick's heart and squeezed it. An irrational jealousy burned his mind. The guy who'd let her down didn't deserve being loved and cherished. He'd had something precious and wasted it. Something in Nick fiercely rebelled at that man being *the only one* in Merry's life.

Merry... Damn it! The name had an insidious attraction. Nick silently vowed not to use it. It might give Kimberly a happy sense of being linked to her *real* father, which was fair enough, but Nick instinctively recoiled from using *his* special name for her. Meredith, he thought, forcefully stamping on the strong appeal of *Merry*.

"What happened?" Kimberly's question snapped Nick's attention back to her. She was frowning, looking puzzled, worrying over her mother. "I mean...he shouldn't have left you. How could he? Especially when you were going to have his baby."

No wool pulled over Kimberly's eyes, Nick thought with approval. She'd gone straight to the crux of the matter. It would do Meredith good to see the past from a less rosy-eyed, emotional perspective.

"Sometimes things happen that we have no control over, Kimberly."

The rueful reply twisted him up again. "What things?" he demanded, more harshly than he meant to. His insides writhed with embarrassment.

Meredith Palmer's personal past was none of his business. It was okay for Kimberly to ask about it but he should be keeping his mouth shut.

Those soul-tugging green eyes fastened on his and he had the weird sensation they were drawing on his mind, looking for an answer that would make sense to him.

"He was twenty-two," she said quietly. "When he found out I was only sixteen, he thought he should wait until I was older. We parted on the understanding of contacting each other at Christmas each year."

"But when you found out you were having me, didn't you tell him?" Kimberly queried. "Wasn't that more important than waiting for the next Christmas?"

Nick felt a sense of release as Meredith Palmer turned her gaze to his niece. It was like a cobweb of tingling threads being withdrawn. So conscious was he of the extraordinary effect, he barely heard her reply.

"I tried. Circumstances had changed for him. He'd gone overseas and I had no way of making contact."

"What about when the next Christmas came?" Kimberly pressed. "Did he write?"

A wistful shake of the head. "Not to my knowledge. If he wrote, the letter went astray."

Kimberly was visibly distressed by the tragic outcome of that possibility. She searched for a way around it. There was none, yet the pleading for some other resolution was in her voice as she cried, "He didn't ever come back to you?"

It was wrong for him not to. So obviously, hurtfully wrong. Kimberly needed some mitigation for his abandonment of her mother. It was all too plain to Nick that to her young, trusting mind, a love such as Meredith had described, should have an answer. He should have come. But that emotional certainty didn't change anything. It only raised a tension that tore at all of them.

Meredith Palmer summoned a wry smile in an effort to dissipate it. "Time moves on and people move on, Kimberly. They meet other people."

The philosophical reply didn't satisfy. Nick found it too tolerant and forgiving. Kimberly heaved another sigh, this one of deep discontent. She didn't like the story left dangling in no man's land.

"But you're so beautiful, Merry!" she protested. "I don't see how he could forget you."

Nick saw the flicker of pain on Meredith Palmer's face and suffered a wave of guilt for having encouraged this line of questioning. Of course she would feel obliged to answer Kimberly, wanting her daughter's sympathy and probably frightened of condemnation. But on their part, shouldn't curiosity take second place to compassion? God only knew how rough a time she'd been through. They should let the past rest and get on with the present.

And the future.

He quickly inserted, "There could have been other reasons why your real father never came back, Kimberly. Since none of us know, let's leave it at that, shall we? I'm sure Miss Palmer would like to talk of happier things."

"Oh!" Kimberly squirmed as her mind flashed through other scenarios, probably remembering last year's fatal car accident. "Uncle Nick said you run a florist business," she said in a gush of relief at having seized on a less sensitive subject. "What's your favourite flower?"

Flower Power provided bright conversation. Nick sat back and let it flow, discreetly observing the fascinating play of expression on Meredith Palmer's face, the eloquent body language encompassing the listening tilt of her head, the graceful hand gestures, the concentrated interest, the warm inviting smiles. Her whole being was reaching out to her child with every breath she took, every word she spoke.

Kimberly was entranced.

Nick wondered what it would be like to have all her passionate intensity focused on him. He fought a constant battle against a tightening in his loins. Desiring a woman so much on such little acquaintance was a new experience and he wasn't sure he liked it. Being in control was second nature to him. Around this woman, the laws of nature didn't seem to apply.

Again he was tantalised by the question of how her image had been branded on his subconscious and why it emerged in his dreams. She *was* beautiful, though it was more the power behind the beauty that teased Nick's mind. Kimberly had a point in blurting out, *I don't see how he could forget you!* On no acquaintance at all, Nick had found Meredith Palmer so unforgettable she haunted his dreams! Any way he looked at it, that teetered on the supernatural.

He was glad when lunch arrived. Eating was an ordinary human habit. Not that she ate much. Nick forced himself to consume everything on his plate and the lion's share of the salad, as well. It proved, at least to all outward appearances, he was handling everything with ease.

Occasionally Kimberly called on him to comment on some point of the conversation but Meredith Palmer never once tried to draw him into it. He sensed she was wary of him, guarded, perhaps overconscious of his power to call a halt to this meeting and take Kimberly away from her. Or was she as acutely aware of him as he was of her, and hiding it in case it created a problem in future meetings with her daughter?

He was still speculating on this possibility when Kimberly turned to him, her face transparently eager as she asked, "Uncle Nick, is it all right for Merry to come over to the apartment tomorrow? I could show her all my stuff."

"Would you like to, Miss Palmer?" he asked, wanting to make her look at him full-on again. For the past hour he'd received no more than brief, courteous glances, frustrating his need to know if he was right about a mutual attraction.

Her eyes met his and his stomach contracted. Hope burned in their luminous green depths, an anguished hope that begged more from him than a casual invitation. "Yes," she said simply. Then as though belatedly recognising it might be an imposition on his generosity, she flushed and added, "If it won't inconvenience you, Mr. Hamilton."

"You're welcome." It was the truth. On more levels than he cared to examine. He wanted her. Not in his dreams, but in his flesh and blood life. She held the promise of things that demanded exploration.

"Thank you."

Her smile was radiant, bathing him in a pulsing glow of happiness. "Call me Nick," he commanded on a sudden rush of blood to the head. He didn't want distance between them. He wanted... God! It was almost impossible to clamp down on his rioting feelings but he managed some semblance of it, smiling back at her and asking, "May I call you Meredith?"

The sparkling light in her eyes momentarily receded, as though sucked back to some dark place in her soul. It burst on him again so quickly, the slight falter was erased and Nick was showered with pleasure.

"Yes. Please do."

The soft lilt of her voice sang through him, stroking chords and striking harmonies that filled him with a glorious sense of well-being. The sense of starting out on a path that had always been waiting for them was overwhelming.

Kimberly reclaimed her attention, working out the details of tomorrow's visit. Nick didn't care what was arranged. Something special had started between him and Meredith Palmer. He knew it in his bones. The determination to pursue it as far as it could go was burning in his heart. Tomorrow was the next step.

Meredith...maybe when he'd called her by her full name she'd momentarily remembered the guy who'd called her Merry, but she'd come back to him with a burst of positive signals. Nick was fiercely glad that her one great love had walked out of her life and never returned, elated that he had this chance at something unbelievably unique in his experience.

Surely she could put that man behind her now.

Thirteen years had passed. Though she hadn't forgotten him. But Kimberly had hit the nail on the head. How could he have forgotten her? The man had to be a shallow fool, probably breaking hearts wherever he went on his very convenient trip overseas.

Nick reflected, with some irony, that he'd been twenty-two himself, thirteen years ago. And he'd gone off overseas at the same time, having won a grant for further studies at Harvard University in the U.S.

Strange, the little coincidences in life...the man who'd left her...and the man with her now. Had the two of them met? he wondered. Had he been shown a photograph of Merry?

He couldn't recall any such incident.

It didn't really matter.

The woman of his dreams was with him in reality. He didn't care what had happened before. The future was his to make.

CHAPTER EIGHT

MEREDITH took three deep breaths in a vain attempt to calm her nervous excitement before ringing the doorbell to Nick Hamilton's apartment. Its Blues Point location, with views over the harbour, made it prime real estate, way beyond her income bracket. She was about to step into a world of wealth and class and it was difficult not to be daunted by it.

She reminded herself it had always been Nick's background, though she hadn't realised it until she'd gone looking for him at the address he'd given her. Denise and Colin Graham had lived in a magnificent home at Pittwater in those days. It was one of the reasons she'd given up her baby to them, wanting her daughter to have all the privileges she couldn't provide, the same privileges her father had.

Nevertheless, wealth and class couldn't provide mother love and that was what Kimberly wanted now. There was a need to be filled and Meredith was determined to fill it as far as Nick Hamilton would allow. Surely this Sunday brunch had to mean he was willing for them to establish an on-going relationship.

Ever since they'd parted yesterday she'd been

hugging his "You're welcome" comment to her heart.

Welcome in *his* life, too? Was he attracted to her again? Maybe it was too much to hope for. Dangerous, too, if it got in the way of forging a future with Kimberly.

Caution had to be exercised. He'd unbent enough to invite her to call him Nick, but Meredith was not Merry. He didn't remember what they'd shared and it was no use wanting him to. She had to take it from here...whatever came.

Despite the three deep breaths, her pulse was wildly fluttering as she pressed the doorbell. Kimberly must have been prowling near the door, impatient for her arrival. Meredith had barely touched the button before her daughter was in front of her, the entrance to her home swept wide open in eager welcome.

"Hi!" It was a breath of delight, accompanied by a grin from ear to ear. "You made it here in time!"

In time for what? Meredith puzzled. Nick had said brunch was casual and arriving any time after eleven would be fine. Feeling somewhat confused, she asked, "Was I supposed to be here earlier?" A quick check of her watch showed eleven-twenty.

"Oh, no! Everything's perfect," Kimberly assured her and grabbed her hand to draw her inside. "I love that outfit, Merry."

No problem there. Her stretch tights were lime green, printed with white daisies and teamed with a loose white T-shirt. Meredith had chosen her outfit for its appeal to her daughter and bright colours were certainly the order of the day. Kimberly was in orange shorts and a matching midriff top.

"I love what you're wearing, too," she said, smiling warm approval. It would be marvellous to take her daughter shopping one day. Was it too soon to suggest it?

The compliment didn't really register with Kimberly. "They're just old things," she dismissed, hustling Meredith inside and pushing the door shut. Clearly pumped up with excitement, she danced ahead, pulling on Meredith's hand to urge her forward. "Do come on, Merry. They're out on the patio."

Hit by the ultra modern and expensive decor in the open plan living room—black leather, streamlined chrome and glass, collector pieces of art, carpet so plush footprints showed up in it—Meredith was slow to pick up on the critical word. Then a frisson of unease ran down her spine. She stopped dead, halting Kimberly's headlong rush past the designer class dining suite.

"Who are *they?*"

She hadn't been told there would be other guests this morning. She wasn't prepared for it.

Kimberly shrugged as though it was nonconsequential. "It's only Uncle Nick and the woman he goes out with. She dropped in about half an hour ago. Her name is Rachel Pearce."

A lump of lead plunged into Meredith's heart. He was involved with someone else. With a woman who felt comfortable enough in their relationship to drop in whenever she wished.

"I want her to meet you."

No...o...o...o. The silent wail echoed down the chasm that had opened up in Meredith's mind, swallowing the hope she had nursed and spilling an ink-black darkness into her soul.

"It will only take a minute," Kimberly offered persuasively. "Then I'll show you my room."

She had to drag herself out of the pit to focus on her daughter again, seeing her own green eyes looking back at her, wanting her compliance, not realising what was asked had any import to Meredith beyond a casual meeting of two people who didn't know each other.

Her daughter...whom she wanted to keep seeing...so meeting the woman in Nick Hamilton's life was inevitable. Seal off what cannot be, reason dictated. Get on with it. "Do you like her, Kimberly?" Meredith asked softly, needing to know what she was walking into so as not to blunder onto sensitive territory and do herself a damage.

"She's okay, I guess," came the half-hearted reply. Her nose wrinkled expressively. "She sort of talks down to me but she's not nasty or mean.'' Then realising her words might be off-putting, she hastily added, ''You don't have to worry, Merry. She'll be nice to you. Uncle Nick wouldn't like it if she wasn't.''

Her daughter was no fool, Meredith thought wryly. She was certainly wise to the ways of a woman who wanted to keep a man's good opinion. Curiosity, on her daughter's behalf, helped push the pain aside. An assessment of the woman who might be playing a big part in Kimberly's life was necessary if she was to understand the situation and be of any help.

''Well, I guess I'd better meet her,'' she said, practising a smile.

''Great!'' Kimberly enthused. ''She'll probably be dead jealous when she sees how beautiful you are.''

Meredith wasn't sure if her daughter was proud of her or intent on stirring up trouble. Either way, she had little time to think about it. Kimberly was on the march again, pulling her past a luxurious lounge setting to the glass doors that led out to the patio.

A profusion of purple and cerise bougainvillea grew from huge earthenware urns and spilled over the safety wall that edged the spacious outdoors area. Casually arranged on a lovely blue-green slate-covered floor were a dining suite, a couple of occasional tables and three sun loungers in white lace aluminium, comfort provided by royal blue cushions.

Nick Hamilton and a red-haired woman sat at the dining table, cosily chatting to each other. Their heads swivelled at the sound of the doors sliding open and both of them pushed their chairs back and rose to their feet as Kimberly led Meredith out to them. Wealth and class staring her in the face, Meredith thought, mentally building herself a thicker protective wall to ward off their effect on her.

Nick was dressed in a smart, casual Jag ensemble, the steel blue shorts revealing the powerful muscularity of his legs, the loose tomato-red top emphasising the broadness of his chest and shoulders. He was definitely *at home,* albeit in designer leisure wear.

Rachel Pearce, however, could have stepped out of *Vogue* magazine. She was style from head to toe, making Meredith feel like a dropout from a chainstore.

Beautifully tailored white linen trousers teamed with a matching halter-neck top that moulded a perfectly curved figure. The jacket that completed the outfit was hooked over the back of her chair. Silver bracelets adorned her arms and silver hoops hung from her ears, dramatic against the shining copper of her hair and the make-up that emphasised pretty features and polished sophistication.

Her suitability for a man of Nick Hamilton's status and her sex appeal were heart-wrenchingly obvious to Meredith, and that comprised only surface attractions. No doubt she had other qualities that appealed to the man beside her.

"This is my *real* mother," Kimberly announced to the woman, her voice ringing with triumphant satisfaction, as though the reality of a mother could displace any ambitions Rachel Pearce might have for fulfilling a maternal role. Unfortunately, relationships didn't fall into neat black and white patterns.

Nick sighed and gestured a reproof at his niece. "Kimberly, a proper introduction would be appreciated."

"She's all excited, Nick," his companion excused indulgently, one hand touching his arm in a soothing squeeze, a claim of familiarity that spelled out her position. Her smile to Meredith could not be faulted. It was open and friendly, her eyes dancing with interest. "Hello... I'm Rachel Pearce," she said with easy warmth, offering her other hand invitingly.

Meredith took it, adopting the "we aim to please" air she used with a prospective client. "Meredith Palmer. A pleasure to meet you, Miss Pearce."

"Rachel...please," came the laughing reply. "Nick has been calling you Meredith. I hope you don't mind if I do."

Establishing their coupling.

"Not at all." Conscious of not having really acknowledged Nick Hamilton as yet, Meredith made the effort to shift her gaze to him and say, "Good morning, Nick," as lightly as she could.

She caught him perusing her long legs, faithfully and emphatically outlined in lime green. On the instant of hearing his name, his gaze flicked up, the dark eyes sharp and alert and boring into hers with an urgent intensity that made no sense to Meredith. What was he thinking? That she might side with Kimberly against the woman he wanted? Clearly there was a conflict area which needed delicate negotiation. Maybe he was trying to discern if she would be his ally or his enemy.

"Another beautiful day," he said. "It's good to see you, Meredith. Would you like to join us or..."

"Merry wants to see my room," Kimberly answered for her. "I've got all the photo albums laid out on the bed and my swimming trophies and..."

"I see the first claim has been made," Nick broke in dryly.

"Yes. If you'll excuse us..." Meredith said quickly, flashing an appealing smile from him to Rachel Pearce.

"Of course. You must want to catch up on everything,'' Rachel said, her eyes sympathetic, not the least bit jealous of Kimberly's attention.

"We did invite Meredith for brunch, Kimberly," Nick reminded her. "Don't get so involved with showing off that you forget we're supposed to eat, too."

"I've got a bowl of cherries and a big bag of chips. Give us a call when you put on the barbecue, Uncle Nick," she answered breezily.

He rolled his eyes and shot a grin at Meredith that pierced her shield and hammered into her heart. "Doomed to cherries and chips. Be assured I will rescue you."

She managed a laugh, nodded to his companion and took her leave of them with Kimberly, fiercely telling herself once again the past was gone. The love of her life could not be rescued.

"What did you think of her?" Kimberly demanded in a confidence-inviting whisper as they traversed the living room, heading for a hallway.

Meredith instantly adopted neutral ground, wary of repercussions. "I don't know her, Kimberly. If you want my first impression, she's smart and pretty and has a very pleasant manner."

It drew a huff and a grimace. "I don't want Uncle Nick to marry her. He'll have no time for me if he does."

Meredith frowned. "I'm sure that's not true. He cares very much about you."

"She brought over the enrolment forms for PLC. That's *her* old school. She's got Uncle Nick thinking it would be good for me to be a boarder there."

"It is a top-class school," Meredith commented cautiously, aware it was also a highly expensive private school that carried a lot of status, both socially and academically. Students there were definitely privileged, which was what she had wanted for her daughter, though not at the cost of her being unhappy.

"I don't want to be a boarder." It was a sulky, belligerent statement. "She wants me out of the way so she can have Uncle Nick to herself."

That might or might not be true. In all fairness, Meredith had to reserve judgment. She tried to take a middle line. "I thought most boarding schools allowed their students to go home at weekends."

It didn't work.

Kimberly shot her a doleful look.

"What would be the use? She and Uncle Nick go out most Saturday nights. Mrs. Armstrong comes to mind me. I might as well be at the school with the other girls who stay in."

"There is Sunday," Meredith reminded her.

Another grimace. "It's not the same with Uncle Nick when *she's* here."

Kimberly fell into brooding silence as they walked along the hall. Meredith didn't feel equipped to break it in any constructive way. The situation had changed dramatically from what she had imagined it to be earlier this morning.

A prospective stepmother.

Rumblings of discontent from Kimberly.

Areas of conflict rising from the intermingled relationships.

Was she supposed to supply a solution?

What if Nick Hamilton wanted her to establish a good relationship with Kimberly so she could provide a happy alternative to coming home to a stepmother who seemed only to stir resentment?

They came to the room at the end of the hall. Kimberly had her hand on the knob, ready to open the door when she paused, turning to eye Meredith speculatively.

"You know what would be really good?"

"Tell me." Safer to invite than to guess.

She hesitated a moment, then seemed to pick her way carefully as she said, "Uncle Nick is going to invite you to spend the Christmas holidays with us at Pearl Beach. It's on the Central Coast, about two hours from here. Can you come, Merry?"

Christmas with her daughter. She wouldn't let anything get in the way of having that joy. She smiled. "Yes. I'd love to."

"You'll be in the same house with us," Kimberly said with satisfaction. "It's right on the beach, so you'll like it."

"I'm sure I will."

"And Ms. Pearce won't be there."

Meredith made no comment. The Machiavellian glint in her daughter's eyes was disquietening. It was a relief when she grinned and her expression changed to mischievous conspiracy.

"It would be really good if we could get Uncle Nick to marry you instead of her...wouldn't it!"

CHAPTER NINE

THEY strolled along Pearl Beach in the darkening twilight—man, woman, child—and Meredith let herself pretend they were together in the idyllic sense. After all, it didn't matter what she dreamed as long as neither Nick nor Kimberly knew.

It was their first night here, the first of nine nights they would spend in this beautiful place with no one else to please but the three of them. The three of them for Christmas. Tomorrow was Christmas Eve. Tonight was simply for the pleasure of feeling their normal lives were left behind in Sydney and this was the start of a special time.

For her it was, anyway.

This was her family...her child...and the father of her child.

After these holidays...but she wouldn't think about what might happen then. Better to treasure every moment she had with the only two people who were especially dear to her.

Although Nick had brought provisions, now stacked away in the kitchen of the holiday house, they'd gone to the take-away shop in the village and dined on hamburgers and chips, just like any other family who didn't want to bother with cooking after a long, busy day. The walk home along the beach was Kimberly's decision. Meredith suspected it was part of her daughter's plot to promote romantic situations between her and Nick.

She skipped ahead of them, dancing around the scalloped edges of dying waves, still very much a child, perhaps enjoying the fact that her parents were following her, watching her antics, caring about her. Not that Nick knew he was her father, but being her legal guardian was more or less the same. Meredith wondered what he was thinking...feeling.

He was walking beside her, as they'd walked so long ago, sand squelching under their feet, the splash of waves slapping onto the shore, whooshing up and being sucked back, the underlying thrum of the sea in constant motion, a breeze flicking their hair and teasing their nostrils with the fresh smell of salt.

She could feel the heat of his body, almost touching hers. His strong maleness stirred an acute awareness of her femininity and the need to have it complemented. They had once been perfect together. The memory clung, arousing desires she hugged to herself, secretly wishing they could be expressed.

It was strange. The thought of Rachel Pearce had tormented her all week, yet here...maybe it was the sense of distance or the magic of the night...the woman who belonged to Nick's city life just didn't seem real. Only the three of them were real...walking together...listening to the same sounds, all their senses alive to a different world.

"Look at the stars! There are so many!" Kimberly remarked in awe.

"No pollution dimming our view of them," Nick commented.

"That's so unromantic, Uncle Nick."

"Simple truth."

Kimberly huffed her exasperation. None of her matchmaking efforts had borne any fruit so far. Meredith found them intensely embarrassing and Nick pretended he didn't notice the hints and manoeuvrings.

"We're almost home," Kimberly pointed out.

"So we are," Nick agreed dryly.

Their holiday home was a rambling old weatherboard house with verandas running around all four sides of it. Built before any council regulations came into force, it faced directly onto the beach with no reserve in front of it. The foundation pylons were high, ensuring the body of the house remained above shifting sand dunes. Quite a steep flight of steps led up to the veranda overlooking the sea.

"I think I'll go straight to bed," Kimberly announced. "I'm really tired out and I want to get up early tomorrow."

"Bed sounds a good idea," Nick tossed back at her.

She rounded on him. "Not for you, Uncle Nick. It's too early for you." Most emphatic.

"Aren't I allowed to be tired?" he teased.

"You always say you need to wind down first," Kimberly sternly reminded him. "It'd be good for you to have a nightcap before going to bed."

"Mmmh…" Noncommittal.

"One of those Irish coffees you sometimes make," Kimberly suggested enthusiastically. "You could take it out to the veranda and watch the stars and listen to the sea and really wind down."

"That certainly should be relaxing," he mused.

"And Merry could relax with you. She's been busy, too, getting all the flowers organised for Christmas before coming away. You'd like an Irish coffee, Merry."

Not a question. This was pure and simple manipulation.

There was a laugh in Nick's voice as he turned to her and asked, "Would you care to join me in a nightcap on the veranda, Meredith, counting the stars and being lulled by the sound of the sea until we're ready to fall asleep?"

The light tone made it sound harmless. Why not? she thought, wanting to indulge in her private pretence a little while longer. "I'd enjoy that," she answered, smiling to show she understood there was nothing personal in it on his part. It was no more than an agreeable way of ending the evening.

"That's settled then," Kimberly declared with gleeful satisfaction. She literally pranced up the beach toward the house, apparently re-energised. There was no sign whatsoever of being so tired she had to go to bed.

Nick slowly expelled the breath he'd been holding. At last some time alone with her! No woman had ever shielded herself from him so determinedly and consistently as Meredith Palmer. He'd never felt so intrigued nor frustrated in any other person's company. At least tonight he had the chance to get her to unwind with him.

Thanks to Kimberly, the little minx, prodding and plotting to push them into rearranging their lives to give her what she wanted in the most convenient way possible. Her motivations stuck out a mile. One day he would have to teach her about subtlety. With her too obvious schemes she'd been driving Meredith away from him not toward him, as well as forcing him into maintaining a laid-back attitude to counter any feeling of being trapped in an untenable situation.

Now that Kimberly had gone on ahead he decided to tackle the problem so it wouldn't continue to be a running issue. "It's only natural, you know, for her to see us getting together as a neat solution," he said casually.

A perceptible rise in tension. "I'm sorry. It must make things so awkward for you."

"I can ride it. Kimberly's a good kid. She usually sees sense in the end."

An apprehensive look. "Please don't think I'm encouraging her in this…this fantasy."

"Meredith, it's very plain to me you're not," he said dryly.

"I never meant to make trouble for anyone."

He found the anxiety in her voice painful. "You aren't," he quickly assured her. "Please stop worrying."

No relief flashed at him. The silence as they walked on was heavy. He tried to think of what other assurance he could give to ease her concerns. More than anything he needed her to open up to him. Then he'd have something to work with.

"It's easy for you to say that." Her voice was quiet, not accusing yet strained with inner torment. "You have the power to take Kimberly away from me again if it gets too much for you."

The shock of what had been playing on her mind halted him. She stepped ahead. His hand automatically lifted, clasping her shoulder to halt her, too. "You can't think I'd be so heartless!" The words burst from him in horror. He wasn't aware of his fingers digging into her flesh in reflexive recoil from her view of him.

She stood still, absolutely still for several seconds, long enough for him to recollect himself and realise she was holding her breath, frightened to move. He hastily loosened his grip, sliding his hand to her upper arm as he strode forward and wheeled to face her, compelled to dispel her fears.

"Meredith..." Her eyes were unfocused, unseeing, staring straight through him. He grasped her other arm, tempted to shake her, barely restraining the turbulence she stirred in him. "Meredith..."

"What do I know of you...of the man you are now?" Her voice sounded eerily hollow.

An uneasy feeling crawled down Nick's spine. What did she mean...*now?* Had they met in some other life? He shook off the wild idea. Be damned if he was going to get befuddled over supernatural stuff again! This was now and he had to get through to her.

"I'm the same man who came to you ten days ago, wanting to find a way to reunite you and your daughter," he stated vehemently.

Her gaze suddenly sharpened, fastening on his with blazing intensity. "Why? For her sake or yours? It couldn't be mine. I'm a stranger to you. And I don't know what the end is."

The agony of doubt in her voice hit him hard. She had shown him, shown both him and Kimberly where she was coming from, and he hadn't answered her need to know where they were going to. A woman without any legal right to her child, afraid of being cut off again...it sickened his soul that she'd been in such torment while he and Kimberly breezed on with their lives, including her as they wished.

"It wasn't for my sake, Meredith. I came for Kimberly, for a child who wanted to meet her real mother. I didn't know the end then and I don't know it now. It's what you and she decide."

Rejection of his claim twisted across her face. "You know I have no control over this. It all depends on your generosity."

He dropped his grasp on her arms to cup her face, to hold it still, to force her to look into his eyes and see his sincerity. "Then take it from me. I'm prepared to be generous."

"Why?" came the anguished whisper.

"Because I care."

Her eyes searched his in tortured uncertainty. "Care...for me?"

It was on the tip of his tongue to say she moved him as no other woman ever had but he knew it wasn't an appropriate answer at this raw moment. She needed reassurance, a sense of security. Very gently he fanned a finger across her cheek and smiled a soft appeal.

"Is it so impossible for you to believe that I can

feel compassion for the loss you've felt? To want you to know what you should have known as a mother?''

Her lashes swept down. Her throat moved in a convulsive swallow. He sensed her struggle to come to terms with what he'd said. The breeze flicked tendrils of her long hair across the back of his hand. He couldn't resist tucking them back behind her ear. She didn't seem to notice.

''It was good of you to invite me here with you,'' she said stiltedly, as though pushing the words out, reciting them as a grateful and well-mannered guest might. ''I'll try not to be a...a burden on you.''

The sense of displacement that haunted her twisted his heart. ''Meredith...just be yourself,'' he implored, trying to instil some confidence in the beautiful person she was. ''Enjoy this Christmas.'' He hoped it would go some way to making up for all the empty Christmases she'd had.

She bit her bottom lip. Her shoulders rose and fell as she inhaled deeply and expelled the long breath. Her lashes slowly lifted. Tears glistened in her eyes. ''Is it only for Christmas?'' she asked huskily.

He didn't know what she meant. He frowned, trying to follow her thoughts. ''I hope you'll enjoy the rest of your life, Meredith,'' he said, genuinely wanting her to be happy, distressed that he'd inadvertently given her cause for tears.

"No. You said...Kimberly wanted her real mother for Christmas."

"And you thought..." Horror at his blind insensitivity struck him again. "Oh, hell! It might have started like that, Meredith, but I honestly see it going on for the rest of your lives."

The tears spilled down her cheeks.

He couldn't bear it. He wrapped her in his arms and hugged her to him, wanting to comfort, wanting to impress on her that the terrible loneliness she had known was over. The silent weeping broke into convulsive sobs, her body trembling as she fought to stifle them.

"It's all right," he murmured, stroking her hair, easing her head onto his shoulder. "You've held too much in for too long. It's all right to cry."

The stiffness collapsed. She sagged against him as though suddenly released from unbearable strain and the weeping was deep and uncontrolled.

Nick ached for her, hating the burden she'd carried around in her mind. The urge kept surging through him to tell her she'd come home now and there was nothing more to worry about. He'd take care of her. He'd take care of everything for her and she'd never be unhappy or alone again.

Madness.

But it didn't feel mad. It felt right. Maybe it was the protective male being fired in him, but he'd never felt anything so strongly before. He was hold-

ing her and the desire to hold on to her forever
suffused his entire being. Meredith, he thought, the
woman he'd been waiting for. She'd finally come
to him, out of his dreams and into real life.

Merry...the name slipped into his mind, tantalising with its emotional pull, yet too associated with
her love for another man for him to use. He
wished...no, he couldn't unwish the past. Without
Kimberly they might never have met.

God! He'd forgotten Kimberly!

The lights were on in the house. She'd gone inside. If she'd witnessed this scene she'd be more
than happy to leave them to it. Not that it meant
what she probably thought, but what the hell! He'd
sort it out with her tomorrow.

Meredith's needs demanded all his concentration
right now. He suddenly realised she had stopped
crying. Probably too drained to move. Or maybe it
felt good to her to be held. By him. He hoped so.

The thought of making love to her crept into his
mind and triggered a sharp awareness of how her
body was fitted to his, the warm feminine softness
clinging to his chest and belly and thighs. The
temptation to run his hand over the curve of her
bottom and press her closer was almost overwhelming. He had to fiercely will the growing tension in
his loins to ease off. It was imperative to soothe
Meredith's fears, not raise more. The last thing he

wanted was to alarm her into being skittish with him again, shying away from any contact.

"Kimberly!"

Her head jerked back as the name exploded off her lips. Agitated hands pushed at him as her gaze swept the area up to the house, her face mirroring shock at having forgotten the presence of her daughter.

"No problem," Nick assured her. "Kimberly didn't stick around. She put the house lights on for us and has probably taken herself off to bed by now."

"Oh!" Her eyes fluttered at him in embarrassment. "I'm sorry..."

"Don't be. I'm sorry we put you in such stressful turmoil. I had no idea you saw yourself on trial. That's not how it is, Meredith, I promise you."

She sucked in a deep breath and expelled it on a long, shuddering sigh. "I completely lost it." Still embarrassed, she started shifting backwards, creating distance between them again.

Rather than lose all contact with her, Nick dropped his embrace, sweeping one arm out as a directive to the house and dropping the other to catch her hand and hold it in a companionable grasp as he started them walking again, smiling encouragement at her.

"What you need is an Irish coffee to unjangle all

your nerves. I can highly recommend it as a restorative as well as a relaxing agent.''

It teased a wobbly smile from her. ''You're very kind.''

''Hold that thought!'' he admonished her with mock gravity. ''No more making me out a callous monster. Okay?''

''Okay.''

She was tagging along with him, letting her hand rest in his. He kept his grip steady, elated at this small victory. ''Once we're settled on the veranda, we'll talk about what you'd like to have with Kimberly. Get it sorted out as best we can.''

Another wobbly smile. ''Thank you.''

''You know, last year with Denise and Colin gone and their deaths happening so close to it, Kimberly and I had a fairly miserable Christmas. This year, because we have you with us...'' A family again, he thought, his grin unashamedly showing delight in the idea. ''...We'll have a merry Christmas.''

Her feet faltered. She stared at him, an arrested look on her face, and Nick started to tingle...everywhere...as though all the Christmas lights in the world had been switched on inside him. Then he realised what he'd said...Merry Christmas...and the primal male inside him rose

rampant, determined to fight his way to her heart.
Me.
Not him.
Me.

CHAPTER TEN

NICK released her hand to let her precede him up the steps to the house. Meredith's heart was pumping so hard her temples throbbed. She grabbed the banister to keep herself steady. It was an act of will to force her quivery legs into the required climbing action.

The way he'd looked at her just now, when he'd said ''Merry Christmas''...it was as though time had tunneled backward. But he didn't know. He hadn't realised. Yet how could he look at her like that without feeling what he'd felt all those years ago? Was it happening again?

Her mind whirled with the eruption of desires from their long, dormant state. Impossible to tuck them away again. They were running rampant, demanding release, demanding expression, crying out against the containment she had enforced. If she just turned, reached out, they would surely be met and answered by the man who'd answered them so magically before.

Then the insidiously dampening thought of Rachel Pearce wormed its way through the chaotic impulses holding reign. However unreal the other woman seemed right now, she did exist in Nick Hamilton's life and they had most likely been lovers for quite some time.

The image conjured up was miserably deflating. But it didn't have to mean he couldn't be attracted to me, she fiercely argued. Or were her senses distorted from wanting him so much? Maybe she had a fevered imagination from having been in Nick's embrace again, wallowing in the sense of belonging to him.

She reached the veranda and started for the door.

"Why don't you stay out here while I make the coffees?" Nick suggested. "Just relax. It'll be my pleasure to serve you."

He was being kind, giving her time to recover her composure after her crying jag. She nodded and managed another smile. "Thank you, Nick."

"Won't be long," he promised.

She watched him go inside, a man who cared about others' feelings, a kind man, no different from the Nick she'd known so intimately. She should have realised those ingrained qualities of character wouldn't change. Had anything, apart from the one vital loss of memory?

Hopeful thinking, she cautioned herself. Rachel Pearce might be left behind in Sydney. It didn't mean she was forgotten. By Kimberly's account, Nick was very much involved with her. It was indicative of trust and confidence that Kimberly's future educational direction was discussed between them and the choice of Rachel's old school had a ring of family continuity about it. While there didn't appear to be any formal engagement, marriage was probably on their minds.

Nevertheless, they weren't married yet.

Was it bad of her to think that? To want another woman's man?

A fiercely primitive wave of possessiveness tore at the uncomfortable scruples as her mind filled with the thought...*he was mine first!*

And he wasn't indifferent to her. Apart from his words of caring, the way he'd held her while she'd wept had demonstrated a very real caring. Then taking her hand afterward, looking at her with that special sparkle in his eyes...her stomach curled, just thinking about it.

What would happen if she told him Kimberly was his child?

Meredith brooded over the question as she wandered down the veranda and settled in one of the cane armchairs they'd brought out from the house earlier this evening. Was it fair to lay that on him? Was it fair that he'd left her with a baby and wasn't there to stand by her when she'd most needed him?

Not his fault, she savagely reminded herself.

It would make him feel guilty if she told him. Did she want him to turn to her out of guilt?

No.

It had to be with love, given freely.

She knew in her heart it wouldn't work otherwise.

If it was going to happen, it would of its own accord, she decided. All she had to do was wait. Having set her course once more, and having been assured by Nick there was no cut-off point with Kimberly, Meredith switched off her mind, letting the sound of the sea fill it with a rhythm that soothed with its constancy, the repetitive roll of water upon land.

"Two Irish coffees coming up."

The announcement heralded Nick's return to the veranda. Meredith's hard-won sense of peace instantly shattered. Her body sprang alive with a prickling awareness as Nick loomed closer, carrying a tray holding two long mugs. Her mind pulsed with irrepressible needs. She tried desperately to get herself under control as he set the tray on the table next to her and subsided into the chair on the other side of it.

"This is the life," he declared with deep satisfaction. "Far from the madding crowd, no pressure decisions to be made. Sun, sand and surf. Can't beat it for a holiday."

That hadn't changed for him, either.

"Is it very stressful, being a merchant banker?" she asked, grateful for his lead into a safe conversation.

"It has its moments. The money markets need to be carefully watched. But I don't let it get on top of me. It's what I'm trained for,'' he answered with the easy confidence of a man who had a long record of success in the financial world.

"Then it was worthwhile going to Harvard."

His head snapped around. "How do you know I went to Harvard?"

Meredith's heart kicked into a panicky beat. The comment had slipped out and now she had to answer for it. She quickly busied herself, stirring the layer of whipped cream into her coffee while her mind frantically sought an acceptable explanation.

If she said Kimberly had mentioned it... Too risky. He could check with her. Impossible to claim reading it in an article. She had no idea if any story had ever been printed on him. What else would serve...except the truth?

"Your sister told me," she said flatly, evading his sharply questing gaze, sitting back in her chair and holding the mug of coffee to her lips, ready to sip.

"Denise? Why would she tell you about me?"

Meredith's brain moved into crisis mode, darting around danger areas with incredible speed. "I wanted to know about the family that would become my baby's family," she said, keeping her tone eminently reasonable.

"I've been meaning to ask you about your connection with Denise. As I see it, this adoption could not have gone through regular channels. Normally there's no contact between the parties."

He wasn't going to leave it alone. She had to satisfy his curiosity without revealing his paternity. Ruthlessly monitoring every step made toward the adoption, Meredith plunged into telling him the barest of facts.

"My stepmother sent me to her sister in Sydney so my pregnancy wouldn't shame her with her friends. The doctor who did my check-ups was also your sister's doctor. I was booked into a hospital which was a regular channel for adoption through a government agency. Your sister knew the person who could arrange for my baby to be adopted by her."

"Are we talking bribery here?"

"I don't know. You asked for the connections. Those were certainly some of the connections made," she stated carefully.

"Go on," he invited tersely, not liking what he was hearing.

"At first, I didn't want to give up my baby."

"Are you saying my sister and this person coerced you?" he broke in again, clearly upset.

Meredith shook her head and sipped the strongly flavoured coffee, needing a suffusion of warmth. He was shocked, angry, and there seemed no point in stirring bad feelings. It was too late to change anything and Denise and Colin Graham had been good parents to Kimberly.

"They put their case," she explained. "I listened and gave it a lot of thought. I couldn't have let my baby go to someone I didn't know anything about. I trusted your sister to do the best she could for my daughter. She agreed to send me the photographs so I'd know something of her life. And that was it. I signed the adoption papers, knowing my baby was going to a better home than I could give her.''

''You were talked into it,'' he muttered, his sense of fairness still frayed.

''I made the choice, Nick,'' she said quietly.

''Denise could be very domineering.''

''She did all I wanted her to do for Kimberly.''

He ruminated on that for several minutes. ''I guess she did,'' he finally conceded. ''Denise was good at mothering. Our parents died when I was a kid and she was more a mother to me than a sister.''

I know, Meredith thought, but she didn't make the mistake of voicing the give-away words this time.

''She and Colin...they were good people,'' he mused sadly.

He was letting it go. She'd done it! He was satisfied.

His gaze swung around to her, dark and disturbed under frowning brows, making her pulse skitter again.

''All the same, it was wrong to keep bargaining with you when you were so vulnerable. As much as Denise craved a child of her own, she shouldn't have done that.''

Meredith took refuge in sipping some more coffee. When no comment was forthcoming, Nick turned his gaze broodingly out to sea. There was a time and a tide for everything, Meredith thought, and the events Nick was questioning were long gone. Nothing could be gained by chewing over them.

"You said we could talk about Kimberly and the future," she softly reminded him.

"Yes." He brightened, sitting up in his chair and reaching for his coffee, his eyes pleased with the new subject. "Tell me what you'd like to do," he invited warmly.

Relief and pleasure danced through her. He was a beautiful man and her heart swelled with love for him. Her whole being clamoured for a resolution to all the unfinished business between them.

"It depends on what plans you've made," she offered cautiously. "Kimberly said you were thinking of sending her to PLC."

"Ah!" He grimaced. "Do I detect some more manoeuvring and manipulation by my devious niece? Has she been bending your ear about being banished to boarding school?"

"Not really." Meredith saw the opportunity to clarify the situation and took it. "She seems more concerned about how she'll fit into your life if you marry Rachel Pearce."

"Marry Rachel?" He frowned. "It's not on. I never said it was on."

Her pulse went crazy. He wasn't committed. She

gulped some more coffee in the hope it would settle her down again.

"In fact, Rachel dropped by last Sunday to give me the enrolment forms for PLC and let me know she'd just remet the one big love of her life the night before."

"Oh!" That information put a different complexion on the picture. Maybe it was pride saying marriage had never been on. On the other hand, if Nick had been deeply wounded last Sunday he'd been amazingly good at hiding it. "That must have come as a shock to you," she said, watching intently for some sign of the effect on him.

"More a surprise." He shrugged. "I was happy for her. The man in question was married the first time around and she'd been fairly cut up about it. He's now in the throes of divorce and wants another chance with her. Rachel was on her way to meet him for lunch when she called in."

So that was why she'd been dressed to the nines! And Nick was now absolutely free of any sense of commitment to her! Meredith was dizzy with elation. It took an enormous effort to concentrate her mind on finding out if he was also heart-free.

"Were you...very attached to her?"

"You mean, did it hurt?" he said bluntly.

"Well..." She winced sympathetically. "You couldn't have been expecting it."

"We were good friends." He smiled without any chagrin whatsoever. "We're still good friends. I would expect Rachel to call on me for a favour and I'd do the same, if need be.''

"That's nice," Meredith murmured, feeling weak with relief.

"She's a nice person. Unfortunately, she tended to rub Kimberly up the wrong way. No natural knack with children.''

This past year would not have been an easy time to win acceptance, Meredith thought, with Kimberly still feeling the loss of the parents she'd known. Rachel had probably met a brick wall resistance.

"Besides which, I think Kimberly had you on her mind," Nick remarked.

The insight surprised her yet instantly made sense. "The other mother figure," she murmured.

"Precisely. She wanted you. And she finally came out with it.''

Meredith sighed her contentment. It was wonderful to feel wanted by her daughter. If only Nick wanted her, too, her life would feel complete.

"She's very happy with you," Nick assured her.

"Yes." She smiled at him, almost bursting with pleasure. "Though no doubt we'll have our differences in times to come.''

He grinned, his dark eyes dancing again, making her heart trip over itself. "Little storms do blow up now and then. It's a matter of weathering them," he dryly advised. "Tell me what you think about sending her to PLC.''

They talked for hours, plotting—as parents do—what might be best for their child, with the reservation that the plans met with Kimberly's approval. They agreed the most important thing was for her to feel secure about them always being there for her. On the other hand, selfish and unreasonable demands were not to be encouraged nor catered to.

It was marvellous, being invited to share the responsibility of parenthood with Nick. Meredith revelled in it. The time passed so quickly she was shocked when he mentioned it was almost midnight and Kimberly would undoubtedly be up early, excited and full of energy.

They went inside together. Excitement and energy were not reserved for tomorrow, Meredith thought ruefully. Her whole body was tingling with the electricity of being super alive. Sleep looked like being an impossibility for quite a while.

She paused at the door of the bedroom allotted to her and smiled at the man she loved. "Thank you for being so generous. Good night, Nick."

"Sweet dreams," he answered, his eyes the colour of dark chocolate.

They will be tonight, she thought as she murmured, "You, too."

Parting from him was a wrench, but they were under the same roof, in harmony with each other, and there was tomorrow, as well as sweet dreams.

CHAPTER ELEVEN

NICK lay on his bed in the darkness, wondering why he was questioning the sense that something incredibly special had entered his life. Meredith Palmer seemed to offer him everything he'd ever wanted in a woman. The problem was, he couldn't be sure how much the dreams of her were influencing him. Was this compelling attraction wish-driven or substantially real?

The feelings she evoked in him were so strong and happening so fast, he'd barely held back the temptation to push the connection as far as he could tonight. He'd grabbed the excuse of Kimberly's early rising tomorrow to keep his desires in check, but holding control of himself had been a close run thing at her bedroom door.

He wanted her. He wanted to hold her and taste her and absorb every part of her and it was killing him to clamp down on the urges raging through him. If there were only the two of them to consider, nothing would hold him back, but Kimberly was involved too closely with this relationship for him to make hasty moves.

The wisest course was to wait. Meredith was not

about to go away. He had to be sure that whatever he did was right for all of them. It was definitely the sensible thing to do. Recklessly throwing caution to the winds was hardly commendable in this situation.

On the other hand, she emitted a power that made nonsense of caution. Each time he was with her he felt drawn into a vortex of passion that stimulated his body and intoxicated his mind. Pulling back to take stock of where they were was more and more a violation of the flow.

Sweet dreams.

The irony was he'd wanted the magic. Now he was feeling it, the experience was both an exquisite pleasure and a torment. For a moment tonight, when she'd mentioned Harvard, he thought they might have met there. However unlikely it was that he could have forgotten it, at least it would have been an answer to how she'd come to infiltrate his dreams.

And there was the other thing she'd said that had struck him as oddly out of place… *What do I know of the man you are now?* Perhaps it referred to what Denise had told her about him, yet it had felt too personal for merely second-hand knowledge. All his instincts were screaming there was something he should know about Meredith Palmer and if he just reached out far enough it would come to him. Yet it hadn't, regardless of how much he twisted and turned in his search for it.

The click of a door opening interrupted his train of thought. Had he imagined it? No. There was the sound again. He listened for the creak of the floorboards along the hall. The old house didn't lend itself to silent walking. The creak came. Someone was afoot. Kimberly or Meredith?

He listened for bathroom sounds. None eventuated. A visit to the kitchen seemed a reasonable alternative. He lay very still, straining to hear the slightest noise that would affirm his guess or identify some other normal activity. The house was quiet and continued to be quiet. No creak in the hall from footfalls returning. The silence stretched on and on, playing on his nerves. Curiosity turned to concern. Nick rose from his bed to investigate.

No lights were on under any of the doors in the bedroom wing. There didn't appear to be any glow of light coming from the living areas, either. He was crossing the main hall that bisected the house when he noticed the front door slightly ajar, letting in a sliver of moonlight.

A sense of unease drew him on. Had an intruder been in and out of the house? It didn't occur to him he was only wearing the boxer shorts he normally slept in, the concession to modesty he'd made when Kimberly had come to live with him. The need to know if it was Kimberly or Meredith or someone else on the move was imperative. Very quietly he opened the door far enough to slide around it.

No one was on the veranda. He stepped out, listening for any movement. Nothing impinged above the sound of the sea. He crossed to the railing, intent on scanning the beach. A figure standing on the waterline directly down from the house caught his eye. *And* stopped his heart as the sense of deja vu swamped his mind.

It was a scene from one of his dreams...the woman standing as still as a statue at the frothing edge of dying waves, her back turned to him, the dark, moody mystery of the sea in front of her, a black velvet sky studded with stars sweeping around and above her. Only the flying strands of hair, flicked out by the breeze from the long fall over her shoulders, added life to her stillness.

As though the breeze carried the essence of her to him, Nick could feel her waiting, yearning for someone to come to her, to join with her and end her long loneliness. The poignant passion of her need swirled into the empty places in his soul and tugged, inexorably pulling him toward her.

Nick was barely conscious of leaving the veranda, his legs automatically pumping down the steps, feet churning through the dry sand of the dunes. His heart was pounding, his mind filled with the compulsion to answer the siren song that he felt was calling to him...only to him...from her.

It was the dream, yet not the dream. This time he could smell the sea, feel the breeze slapping against him and the sand squeezing between his toes...real sensations, exciting him with the promise of a tangible ending. Still there was the eeriness of the action being the same.

As he closed the distance between them she either heard him or sensed him coming and she started to turn, slowly, as though not quite believing he would be there, drawn almost against her will to look...hair whipping across her face, a soft garment wrapping itself around her thighs, her breasts briefly silhouetted, tilted in tantalising womanliness, lending an infinite seductiveness to the sylphlike figure.

Of their own accord, his legs slowed their approach, waiting for her to come full face, waiting for the dream to follow its normal course, anticipating the flash of recognition, the widening of her eyes, the look of wonderment, the joyful welcome that would light her features, shining for him, beckoning him on.

It all happened, as he'd seen it happen countless times, like a video playing over and over in his mind in the dead of night, emerging from some secret place he could neither find nor control.

First the jolt of actually finding he was not a phantom of her mind, then the quiver of delight running through her body, the strong surge of happiness setting her face aglow, her mouth falling slightly open, giving a fuller sensuality to her lips, her eyes huge pools of green, dazzling drowning pools that sucked at his heart.

Now would come the barrier, he thought, the invisible wall he always strained against but couldn't break. Never had he been allowed to reach her.

A clammy sweat broke out on his brow. His hands clenched. The muscles in his legs tautened with all the power he could drive in to them. His heart drummed wild determination. If this was real, nothing could stop him tonight.

He surged forward.

She didn't fade away.

She stood her ground.

He reached out, his hands curling around her upper arms, warm flesh, solid flesh, giving flesh. His chest heaved, fighting the constriction of what felt like steel bands around it. His lungs filled with air. He was alive. And she was alive.

"Who are you?" he cried, his voice hoarse and alien to his own ears, as though possessed by his own dream figure and struggling to emerge into the reality of this night.

She didn't seem to understand. Or the question was irrelevant to her. Her eyes roved his face as though matching it to every detail of a beloved memory, savouring it anew.

He'd reached her, yet in some indefinable way he hadn't reached her. "Who are you?" he cried again in a torment of frustration.

Her eyes fastened on his, wanting him to know, aching for him to know. "I'm Merry," she whispered, "Merry..."

CHAPTER TWELVE

SHE saw the confusion in his eyes and her heart bled for the memory that had been lost. He'd approached her with such an air of purpose and passion, she'd thought it had all come back to him. But it wasn't important. Only the feeling was, and it pulsed from him with a strength that demolished the barrier of time.

Past, present, future...none of it had any meaning. It was all blotted out by the unleashed need surging between them. For Meredith, the magic of coming together again was an irresistible lure. She lifted a hand to his face, instinctively using touch to wipe away the distraction of a name he didn't relate to.

"I couldn't sleep...thinking of you," she murmured, her eyes mirroring the love that was his to take.

"Me? Was it me you were thinking of? Or..." He struggled with the doubt she'd inadvertently put in his mind.

"You, Nick. Only you," she assured him, sliding her other hand up over his bare chest, craving the physical contact she had missed for so long.

130

The flare of desire in his eyes poured a flood of warmth through her veins. He cupped her face, fingers spreading into her hair above and below her ears. His head bent. Her mouth opened to meet his, wanting to feast on his kiss, so hungry for it she went up on tiptoe to accelerate the yearned-for intimacy.

He tasted her eagerness, revelled in it, plundered her mouth with devouring intensity, pent-up need exploding in a passion for every exciting sensation that could be derived from the fierce foray into finding each other, finding and knowing and exulting in the pulsing reality of dreams being fulfilled.

She hung on to his head, fingers clawing through his hair, gripping to keep him with her, driven to a frenzy of possessiveness now that she had him again. He wrapped his arms around her, scooping her into full body contact, electrifying every nerve with an acute awareness of their sexuality...man and woman...wanting what each could give, straining to feel the promise of it.

His hands slid down the arched curve of her back, clutched and kneaded the rounded flesh below it, moulding the softness, fitting her more closely, achingly close to the swollen hardness thrusting from his loins. Her thighs quivered against the taut power of his as desire swirled through her, sensitising her breasts, curling her stomach, stirring the throbbing need to feel him inside her, to hold him there so he would never think of leaving her again, never want to.

His mouth lifted from hers long enough to murmur, "I want you."

"Yes," she answered, her sense of urgency as great as his.

"Now."

"Yes."

"Not here. The grit of sand..."

"Wherever you want."

"The sleep-out on the veranda. We'll be comfortable there."

"Yes."

He broke away, caught her hand, and they ran together in an exhilarating burst of energy, knowing what was to come, the ecstatic freedom of no restraint in their loving, time to explore their pleasure in each other and savour every moment of it. They could have plucked stars from the sky, their spirits were soaring so high, and behind them the sea boomed and crashed in counterpoint to the drum of their hearts.

Nick paused her at the foot of the steps to wash off the sand under a tap positioned there for that purpose, his hands stroking her calves and ankles, caressing her feet and toes. She bent to do the same for him but he grew agitated with her ministrations, quickly turning the tap off and lifting her up, his eyes dark and turbulent as they tensely searched hers.

"You make me feel..."

"What?" she encouraged.

He shook his head. "I want this to be...let me make love to you, Meredith."

A need for control, she thought, but when he swept her off her feet and cradled her against his chest, she wondered if it was some deeply felt male need to claim her as his woman, to impress himself upon her and wipe out any thought of what she'd felt or done with anyone else.

She curled her arms around his neck and nestled her head close to his throat, soaking in the sense of belonging, of having at last come home after years in the wilderness. "I thought you'd never come, but you did," she sighed on a warm gush of happiness. Then, wanting him to know how special he was, "You're the man I've been longing for, Nick."

"Yes." The word burst from him like a shot of steam, pushed from a maelstrom of emotion. His arms tightened around her. "No more waiting, Meredith. That's over."

His voice rang with triumph, as though he'd finally won a hard battle, and like a victor carrying off his reward, he charged up the steps and strode exuberantly around the veranda to the section that had been enclosed for extra sleeping quarters.

The room was stuffy. Nick laid her on the bed,

which was covered with a cotton quilt, then hastily swept around the louvred windows, opening them to the fresh night air. Meredith smiled at his caring for her comfort but her smile was swallowed by a tidal wave of tingling excitement when he dropped his shorts and straightened up, breathtakingly male in his nakedness.

She quickly pushed herself into a sitting position, her hands scrabbling at the short silk shift she'd worn to bed earlier in the night. Wanting to be free of all barriers between them, she dragged it off and hurled it aside, just before he reached her.

He swooped to lift her up, standing her on the edge of the double bed, hooking his hands into the briefs she'd put on before going down to the beach. He paused, breathing hard, his gaze fastened on her breasts, so enticingly close to his face.

Her nipples instantly puckered in response. They were level with his mouth and the temptation to lean forward, to feel his lips encircling them... She moaned with pleasure as he took them, one and then the other, licking, sucking, tugging, drawing on her desire and embellishing it a hundredfold with his.

Excitement pumped from her breasts and streamed wildly to the apex between her thighs. She clutched his shoulders for support as he drew her briefs down, frantic to work her legs out of them so he wouldn't have to bend, wouldn't have to stop the glorious momentum of intensely satisfying sensation.

Her breasts had been made for this and she'd missed having it with the baby she'd borne him, the natural bonding she'd been denied. But Nick wasn't denying her. He was loving her as she'd yearned to be loved, no holds barred, completely and passionately. She cradled his head, cherishing him, caressing the nape of his neck, pressing kisses over his hair.

His hand softly cupped the silky mound below her stomach and she rejoiced that her legs were now free to move apart for him, to invite and welcome his touch, needing it, wanting it, seething with anticipation for it. He stroked her with exquisite gentleness, slowly, seductively, arousing a sensitivity that quivered and craved for more. The slick sweet caresses became unbearable and she clawed his back in a fever of urgent need.

"Nick..."

The groaned plea was enough. An arm crushed her close as he knelt on the bed and lowered her into position for him. Then he reared back, looming over her, his magnificent body taut, every muscle strained with the power of his manhood.

His eyes blazed with a wild exultation as he thrust himself inside her, tunneling fast and deep, and she arched to entice the whole glorious fullness of him, loving its passage, loving the thrilling sensation of its intimate journey to the centre of her inner world.

Only he had ever joined her there and when he reached the innermost rim of it, she wound her legs around him to hold him there, squeezing tight in an ecstasy of possession.

A guttural cry of fierce satisfaction broke from his throat. His arms burrowed under her shoulders, raising her. His mouth came down on hers with ravaging force, invading, possessing, passionately pursuing the deepest sense of union with her. It was wild, beautiful, intense, the penultimate sense of mating.

When her muscles relaxed he pulled his mouth from hers and concentrated all his energy on repeating his first climactic entry, sliding back to plunge again and again, building a rhythm that threshed her into another peak of sweet bliss, and still he went on, riding from crest to crest, pushing the pleasure up a scale of intensity until no more was possible and he spilled the driving force of his need for her, filling her with the exquisite warmth of final fusion.

She took his spent body in her arms, stroking the shuddering muscles into gentle relaxation. Flesh of my flesh, she thought, remembering the baby they'd made and wondering if it would happen again. Would he like it to? Was she assuming too much from one night of loving?

No, it was more than that. Much more. She was certain now he felt all that she did. It hadn't gone away. It had been waiting for her.

Merry... The name kept echoing through Nick's mind as though it belonged to this moment, belonged to the incredible magic of their coming together.

"Meredith..." he said out loud, trying to drive away the echo, override it.

"Yes?"

The husky answer forced him to think of an appropriate reply. Surely to God she'd given him more of herself than she'd given to any other man. It was wrong to confuse this with the spectre of her lost love.

"I could not have dreamed what we've just shared," he murmured, raising himself from her embrace to brush his lips over hers in tender tribute to her generous loving. "It goes beyond dreams."

He rolled onto his side, taking her with him, tucking one arm around her so she lay on his chest, her legs still entangled with his in close intimacy. She felt so right, perfect, as though she'd been made especially for him. How could she have loved another? There'd never been any other woman like her for him.

"It's a miracle," she whispered, her warm breath fanning his skin, making it tingle. "A Christmas miracle.'' He could hear the happy smile in her voice.

Christmas...

Merry Christmas...

The special name stirred an unease, a sense of wrongness he tried to resist, but it persisted. He remembered watching the grieving look on her face, hearing the sad heartache in her voice as she'd recounted how Kimberly's real father had come to call her *Merry*.

How was it then that she'd said to him tonight, *You're the man I've been longing for?*

They'd only met a little over a week ago.

Yet her other words to him also suggested waiting for a much longer span of time...

I thought you'd never come.

Haunting words...focused on him, yet not making any real sense in the context of their short acquaintance.

Her being in his dreams all these years made no sense, either.

He stroked the long silky hair he'd seen so often in those dreams and never been allowed to touch. He played it through his fingers, real hair, as real as she was. She snuggled into a more comfortable position and sighed her contentment. After passion, the peace, he thought. Sweet dreams...

He ran his fingertips over her back, loving the satin texture of her skin, the soft curves of her body.

She was beautiful, inside and out, just as he'd always felt she would be, his fantasy woman come to life. And still he didn't know how the fantasy had begun.

He cast through his memory, trying to recall how far back it had gone. Not school days. Not during his years at Killara Business College. Then there was that blank spot before he went to Harvard, due to that damned surfboard cracking his skull.

It had taken him a while to get his brain back in order to continue his studies for the career he'd been aiming for, trying to recollect things he knew he should know. And yes, he remembered now. The dream had been part of that. He'd put it down to some subconscious manifestation of his frustration. Over the years he'd interpreted it differently, linking it to other things, but it had started then.

After the blank spot.

A nasty little frisson ran down Nick's spine. His mind instinctively shied away from the thought that hit it. But it stuck.

The blank spot incorporated the Christmas period.

Thirteen years ago.

CHAPTER THIRTEEN

A TAPPING on the door woke Meredith. She came alert with a jolt, her head whipping around to find Nick. He wasn't with her. Then she realised this wasn't the sleep-out on the veranda. She was back in her own bedroom. Alone.

"Are you awake, Merry?" Kimberly's voice!

Awake and stark naked! If Kimberly took it in her head to come in... Meredith's agitated gaze finally fell on the nightie and briefs lying across the foot of the bed. She snatched them up and quickly pulled the nightie over her head, struggling to get her arms into the holes. "Yes?" she called, shoving her briefs under the pillow.

"Uncle Nick said if we're to buy a decent Christmas tree, we'd better get moving or the best ones will all be sold."

Nick was up and about! What time was it? She checked her watch. Five to nine. Shock galvanised her into action. She threw off the bedclothes and raced to the wardrobe.

"Sorry I overslept, Kimberly. I'll be right out. Is the bathroom free?"

"Yes. We're all ready."

Almost nine o'clock. Kimberly had probably been up since six. Or earlier. If they'd still been in the sleep-out... Thank heaven Nick had thought of what might happen in the morning. She must have been dead to the world when he'd carried her back here.

She shoved her arms into the silk wraparound that matched her nightie, then quickly grabbed fresh underclothes and the yellow shorts and top she'd planned to wear today. Flushed, her heart racing, she dashed to the door, wrenched it open, and almost ran straight into Kimberly who was still lingering there.

"Oh! I really am sorry, Kimberly. You should have woken me earlier," she rattled out.

"It's okay." A happy grin flashed across her face. "Uncle Nick said you were up really late talking." Her eyes danced with how pleased she was with such promising proceedings from her artful manipulation. "Did you have a good time, Merry?"

Meredith's flush deepened, burning her cheeks. "Yes, I did. I'd better hurry." She sidestepped and headed for the bathroom, acutely aware that the musky smell of their lovemaking was still clinging to her.

"Uncle Nick said it was the best time he'd ever had," Kimberly crowed triumphantly.

Meredith paused with her hand on the knob, her

heart leaping with joy. She smiled back at her daughter...his daughter. "That's nice."

"Yeah," she drawled feelingly. Her eyes sparkled. "And he said he wasn't going to marry Rachel Pearce, so things are going really good."

"Well, I'm glad you're relieved of that worry," Meredith said lightly.

Kimberly surveyed the mussed state of her mother's hair with a critical eye. "You can take your time, Merry," she advised. "We'll wait for you."

Meredith sailed into the bathroom on a wave of pure happiness. *The best time he'd ever had.* Her, too. The very best. Better than before because there was nothing in the way now. Not her age. Not his career. No disapproving family from either side. And their daughter was only too eager for them to come together. It couldn't be more perfect.

Mindful of not spending too long under the shower, Meredith, nevertheless, took a deep, sensual pleasure in soaping her body all over, remembering the magical feelings Nick had aroused in her last night. Sometimes, over the years, she had wondered if she was making the memories better than how it had really been. It wasn't so. If anything, they had dulled. What she had experienced with Nick last night was everything she had remembered and more.

Having switched off the shower and towelled herself dry, Meredith wasted no time in dressing. It was a big bathroom with plenty of bench space and she'd stored her vanity bag in the cupboard under the washbasin. She quickly pulled it out and unzipped it, removing the items she needed.

Kimberly had been right about her hair. The salt air and the breeze had made a mess of it, forcing her to wash it. She wielded a hair dryer and brush to best effect as fast as she could. Lipstick and a touch of eyeliner was enough make-up for the beach.

Confident she was now presentable enough to satisfy her daughter's need for her to look attractive, she raced back to her bedroom to dump her discarded clothes and pick up her camera. Buying their first Christmas tree together was too important an event not to capture on film. Meredith wanted to record everything about this Christmas.

As she crossed the hall she heard Kimberly and Nick bantering with each other in the kitchen. Meredith smiled over their easy give-and-take manner. Little storms might blow up now and then, as Nick said, but they shared a solid familiarity and an understanding that would not be shaken for long. She reminded herself to re-open the PLC issue with Kimberly, now that Rachel Pearce was no longer a factor in the equation.

When she stepped into the kitchen the conversation stopped, two pairs of eyes instantly swinging to her, making her pulse skip into a faster beat with the keen intensity of their interest.

"Oh!" Kimberly beamed approval at her. "You look lovely in yellow, Merry. Doesn't she, Uncle Nick?" An arch look at him.

"Better than sunshine," he obliged, smiling, but Meredith sensed an element of strain behind the smile, a volley of questions that couldn't be asked in front of Kimberly.

"Thank you," she said brightly to both of them, then directly to him, "And thank you for being so considerate of me."

He relaxed a little, his eyes softening with a caring that curled around her heart. "You were obviously exhausted. I hope you slept well."

"Too well. I wish I'd woken earlier." With you, she telegraphed to him, flushing a little as she mentally stripped his navy shorts and white T-shirt, remembering the magnificent power of his body and how it had felt, joining with hers.

"We have many days ahead of us." It was a blazing promise. "There's coffee simmering on the hotplate. Would you like a cup?"

"We kept you some muffins, too," Kimberly chimed in, rushing to set a plate for her.

"Is there time? I don't want us to miss out on a good Christmas tree," Meredith said quickly.

"Looking after you is more important," Nick declared, and the determined look in his eyes brooked no argument.

He waved her to a chair at the kitchen table and Meredith took it, happy to be looked after. She had been looking after herself for so long, she revelled in the feeling of being part of a family—her very own family—who cared about her.

"Uncle Nick and I are going to make this Christmas really special for you, Merry," Kimberly announced, giving her two muffins as Nick poured the coffee. "It's to make up for the ones when you didn't have anybody."

A rush of emotion brought tears to her eyes. She hastily blinked them away and smiled at her daughter. "It's already special."

The best, the very best, she thought blissfully, lifting her gaze to Nick as he set her cup of coffee beside her plate. His eyes mirrored the memories of last night's lovemaking, stirring an embarrassing but secretly exciting range of physical sensations.

The inner muscles that had held him so intimately spasmed in remembered delight and she barely stopped herself from squirming on her chair. She could only hope her bra hid the sudden hardening of her nipples. At least the quiver of her stomach was something that could be settled. She picked up a muffin and munched through it, sipping coffee to wash it down.

Nick engaged Kimberly in conversation while

Meredith was busy breakfasting. Watching the two of them together, so alike in more ways than they realised, it occurred to her she should re-think her decision to leave the past in the past. It felt wrong for Nick not to know he was Kimberly's father. She shouldn't keep such a special, flesh and blood bond from him. From either of them. They both had a natural right to know.

Telling him was not going to be easy, particularly after she had skated over the facts of the adoption last night. Her reasoning for holding back had seemed right at the time, not wanting to burden him with a truth he'd find disturbing and painful, considering the part his sister had played in taking responsibility from him, the long-played deceit that had denied him his true relationship with his own child.

However, the circumstances were different now. Nick felt the same about her as he had all those years before. Rachel Pearce was out of the picture. Meredith decided she wouldn't be putting any sense of obligation or guilt on him now they had come together again. No blame was attached to him for what had happened. He would surely understand that.

He would help her tell Kimberly. Doing it together—both of her real parents—would probably be the least traumatic way, with explanations smoothed by putting more emphasis on the future than the past. She would discuss it with Nick tonight. After they made love. Meredith smiled to herself. Nothing could go badly wrong when the feeling between them ran so strongly.

"Have you had all you want, Merry?" Kimberly asked eagerly.

Meredith promptly rose from her chair and picked up her camera. "Ready to go."

"Great! Let's move!" She took Meredith's free hand and led her toward the door. "Come on, Uncle Nick! We can get a bigger tree this year because there's three of us to carry it back."

Meredith shot him a laughing glance and was surprised by the grim look on his face. His eyes caught hers and he instantly lightened his expression, though not quite enough to completely erase the dark turbulence she saw in them. Something was troubling him. Something he didn't like. She wondered about it as they left the house and took the walk through the nature reserve to the village.

By the time they reached the esplanade she'd dismissed any concern over it. Kimberly was trying to tease out of Nick what he'd bought her for Christmas and he had them both laughing over his outlandish tales of shopping for the perfect gift.

He'd decided against the five thousand piece jigsaw because Kimberly was bound to lose some pieces in the jungle that was her bedroom. Since she had never shown an interest in stitching a fine seam, the super-duper sewing machine seemed bound to be wasted. And so on and so on.

A table-top truck, loaded with Christmas trees, was parked directly opposite the general store. A range of sizes had been propped against the vehicle and an enterprising salesman was doing a brisk trade. As soon as one tree was sold, a helpmate lifted another down to take its place. Meredith was reassured the choice had definitely not been left too late.

Kimberly and Nick strolled slowly down the row, assessing the merits of the trees on display, pausing here and there to stand trees upright, wanting to look at their overall shape. Meredith hung back and snapped photographs of them until Kimberly protested.

"Gosh, Merry! You're as bad as Mum, taking millions of photos of everything. You're missing the fun of choosing."

The words rolled out naturally and Meredith thought nothing of them, content to put her camera away and join them. Nick, however, reacted strongly.

"Take as many photographs as you want, Meredith," he commanded, the dark turbulence flaring into his eyes. He turned sharply to Kimberly. "You know about the packet of photographs Denise sent to Meredith."

She nodded, disturbed by his abrupt change of mood.

"Denise sent them every year. So once a year, your real mother received an update of your life. Just once a year, Kimberly. And that's all she knew of you."

The emotional emphasis laced through the words struck Meredith dumb. She hadn't realised he'd been so deeply affected by the arrangement she'd made with his sister.

"The walls of Meredith's bedroom in her apartment are covered with those photographs," he went on, relentlessly beating out the truth of what she'd missed in giving up her baby. "The best of them are enlarged to see you all the better, everything about you..."

"Nick..." It wasn't necessary to tell Kimberly this, to make her feel guilty for something she wasn't a party to.

An almost savage tension emanated from him as he threw her a fierce look. "She should know how it was for you."

"It was my choice."

"At sixteen?"

"Please..." Her hand fluttered an agitated appeal. "It's over now." She looked at her daughter and smiled to take away the distress Nick had stirred. "You're right, Kimberly. It's better being with you than having photographs."

It was true. She didn't need photographs anymore. She had the real-life experience to enjoy. She walked over to her daughter, put her arm around her shoulders and gave a gentle hug. "Which tree do you like?"

Soulful green eyes looked up at her. "I thought of you, too, Merry. All this year. Ever since I knew of you. I wished I had a photo to see what you looked like, but I didn't have anything."

"I know. It's awful, not knowing, isn't it?" Meredith said in soft sympathy.

She nodded. Her expression turned anxious. "Don't be mad at Uncle Nick for telling me. I'm glad he did, Merry. Now I know you always cared about me."

"I'm not mad at him, Kimberly. He was just showing he cared." She held out her hand to him and willed him to take it. "Thank you, Nick."

He sighed, his eyes wry as his fingers curled around hers and his thumb stroked over the hyperactive pulse at her wrist. "A loving mother deserves no less. How about lending me your camera and I'll take some photos of you and Kimberly choosing the tree? *I'd* like them."

She laughed and handed him the camera, relieved that peace and goodwill had been restored.

Nevertheless, it concerned her that he'd been so upset about the photographs. How much more upset might he be tonight if she told him the full truth? It was Christmas Eve. She didn't want this Christmas spoiled. Maybe it was better to leave telling him everything until more time together built a comfort zone and the past was less sharp than it was now.

Or would that make it worse?

How could she continue to be intimate with him while hiding such a big secret?

Meredith fretted over the decision while she and Kimberly selected a tall tree with the most symmetrical shape. They posed on either side of it for Nick to take his photograph. Once the tree was paid for, they set off for home again, the three of them holding part of the long trunk to keep the branches off the ground.

A family, Meredith thought.

Except two of them didn't know it.

The sense of family was such a happy feeling, the kind of feeling everyone should have at Christmas time. She'd keenly felt the loss of it over the years. Nick and Kimberly must be feeling loss, too, with Denise and Colin Graham gone. Would revealing the truth make it better? Letting them know they still had a very real family? Or would she be destroying memories they held dear?

It's awful, not knowing... The words she'd spoken to Kimberly slipped back into her mind. It was the ultimate truth.

She had to tell Nick.

Tonight.

Then they could both figure out how to tell Kimberly.

CHAPTER FOURTEEN

IT WAS killing him, not knowing. Twice now he'd unsettled Meredith with his brooding over it. Not that she knew what was eating up his mind, and he couldn't just blurt it out. If he was wrong, she would think him mad, connecting himself to the lover who'd fathered Kimberly. He didn't want to confuse her feelings for him. But...he had to know!

Nick paced the living room, impatient for the necessary time to himself to try telephoning his old friends. If anyone would know the critical details of what had happened to him that Christmas thirteen years ago, Jerry and Dave had the inside track. As far as he knew, they'd been with him from start to end of that long vacation.

The tree dominating the corner of the room caught his eye and he stopped, struck by the irony of it all. Another Christmas. Tonight they'd be hanging the decorations on it, making merry.

Merry...

He shook his head, wanting this burden lifted. As soon as Meredith and Kimberly reappeared in their swimming costumes he would send them off to the

beach ahead of him. And damn his old friends to
hell if they could not be reached!

"Great tree, isn't it, Merry?"

Nick spun around. They were in the doorway.
The sight of Meredith in a body-hugging white
maillot, cut high to her hips, took his breath away.
Her skin was tanned to the colour of golden honey
and glowed like silk, compelling the need to touch.
And her legs, her beautiful long legs...the feeling
of them winding around him, tangling intimately
with his was instantly triggered again, setting his
heart pounding, pumping desire into a flood of
wanting.

"You haven't changed into your swimmers."

Kimberly's accusing voice dragged his gaze to
her. "I put them on under my shorts earlier," he
answered distractedly.

"Well, come on then," she urged.

"I'll follow you. I've just remembered a call I
should make."

She groaned. "Not business on Christmas Eve!"

"I won't be long."

"But we need you to bring the windsurfer
down."

He shook his head. "Not enough breeze for it
yet. Best to wait until after lunch. We'll try it then."

A disappointed sigh.

Meredith's hand gently squeezed Kimberly's

shoulder. "Let's not hassle Nick. I'm dying for a swim."

Kimberly's face broke into a cheeky grin. "Last one into the water is a rotten egg."

She dashed off with Meredith in laughing pursuit.

Nick was inexorably drawn to follow as far as the veranda, watching the two of them pelting over the sand. Meredith...the woman of his dreams, gloriously real and tangible and part of his life now. Kimberly...her black ponytail swinging, so many likenesses to his side of the family. Was she his daughter?

He watched them run into the surf, squealing and laughing and heart-wrenchingly happy with each other. If Meredith had missed out on this for all these years because of... Nick's hands gripped the veranda railing hard as a savage sense of loss tore through him.

He had to know.

He strode back into the house, heading straight for the telephone in the kitchen. There'd been no answer from either of the calls he'd made in the early hours of this morning. With it being the Christmas weekend, Jerry and Dave could be anywhere.

None of them was in regular contact, Jerry's work having taken him to Melbourne, and Dave having married in England and settled in London. They exchanged Christmas cards and met for a drink or dinner on the rare occasions they were in each other's cities. Nevertheless, the old sense of mateship was always quickly revived and Nick knew they would help if they could. He fiercely willed for one of them to be home.

He tried Jerry's number first.

No answer.

Frustration rose several notches. He mentally calculated the time in London. Around two in the morning. He didn't care. The need to know overrode every other consideration.

He dialled the international digits and waited, tension screwing up his stomach as the calling beeps repeated their pattern an excruciating number of times. Relief whooshed through him at the clatter of a receiver being fumbled off the hook.

"Dave?" The name exploded off his lips.

"Yeah. Who's this?" Voice slurred with sleep.

"Dave, it's Nick. Nick Hamilton. Sorry to…"

"Hell, man! Do you know what time it is over here?"

"I know but I couldn't get through before."

"Christmas…lines are jammed." The resigned mutter was followed by more alert interest. "So what's up?"

"This is very important to me, Dave. I need your help."

"Right! You've got it." No hesitation.

Nick took a deep breath. "Remember the trip we

went on when we finished college? The one where I ended up in hospital with a cracked skull.''

"Sure I remember it. We hit all the great surfing beaches, right up the coast to Tweed Heads, which was where you copped it.''

"Tell me the beaches, Dave.''

"You ring me up in the middle of the night to find out about beaches?''

"No, it's more than that. I need you to fill in that time for me. It's a blank to me, Dave. Help me with it. Please?''

"Okay. Let me think. Umm...first we stopped off at Boomerang near Forster. Great surf. We even had a school of dolphins swim in one day...''

"Next beach,'' Nick pressed.

"That'd be Flynn's at Port Macquarie.''

"After that?''

"South West Rocks, east of Kempsey.''

"And then?''

"Sawtell. Near Coff's Harbour.''

Coff's Harbour!

Nick swallowed hard. "Dave, did I get tied up with a girl in Coff's Harbour?''

"Ah-ha! Woman trouble! Come back to haunt you, has she?'' Salacious interest.

Nick closed his eyes. Dave couldn't have spoken a truer word than *haunt*. "So there was someone,'' he pressed on, determined to pin everything down.

"Sure was! You were head over heels, man! No

way were you going to leave her. You told us we could travel on if we wanted, but you'd found something a hell of a lot better than surfing beaches, and wild horses couldn't drag you away.''

"So why didn't I stay?"

"Her old woman told you she was only sixteen. A bit young for what you two were getting up to, old son. In the end you saw sense and we travelled on. Put a spike in your usual good humour, though. You shouldn't have taken that spill at Tweed Heads, you know. Your mind simply wasn't on surfing after Coff's.''

It fitted. Yet still he needed the final clincher. "What was her name, Dave?"

"Her name...damned if I can remember."

"Try. Try very hard,'' Nick urged, his heart hammering painfully.

"Don't know that I ever knew,'' Dave mused. "You had a special name for her." He laughed. "Certainly wasn't her real name.''

"Do you remember it?"

"Sure!" He laughed again. "A good one for this time of year, Nick.''

"Tell me."

"Merry Christmas. That's what you called her. Merry Christmas.''

CHAPTER FIFTEEN

NICK jotted down the score, gathered up the playing cards and shuffled them. He looked tired. He'd been rather quiet—almost distant—all evening, only rallying out of his abstraction to respond to Kimberly's demands on him. Meredith hoped he wasn't too tired to stay up with her after Kimberly went to bed.

It had been an active day; swimming, windsurfing, setting the Christmas tree up and decorating it. Besides which, he couldn't have had many hours' sleep last night. He'd been up early with Kimberly this morning. What would she do if he suggested they retire early?

"This is definitely the last hand, Kimberly," he warned as he dealt the cards around the table. "Win or lose."

"But I'm much too excited to go to bed yet, Uncle Nick," she protested, jiggling around in her chair.

The gin rummy score had been seesawing between them and Nick was in the lead at the moment. Meredith was not in the running to win. Her playing had lacked concentration. She was too distracted, thinking about how best to reveal the truth to Nick.

"You've had more than a fair go," he pointed out. "You asked to stay up until *Carols By Candlelight* was finished on the TV, remember?"

"It's only just finished."

"A deal is a deal, my girl."

She huffed and sorted her hand of cards. "I'd better win, then."

Much to her delight, and Meredith's secret relief, she did. Or Nick let her. Either way, there was no more argument about bedtime. She danced around the card table, crowing triumphantly about her victory, gave Nick a hug and a kiss good night, did the same to Meredith, looked longingly at the presents piled under the Christmas tree, then broke into a chorus of "Jingle Bells" as she headed off to her bedroom.

"Hardly a lullaby," Meredith commented, expecting Nick to smile.

He didn't. "Let's clear up," he said quietly. "Get it out of the way."

She was instantly aware of tightly held restraint. The relaxed air he had maintained with Kimberly was gone. The inward tension coming from him was so strong, it plunged her into a turmoil of doubt. Was he regretting rushing headlong into an involvement with her?

She looked searchingly at him but his gaze was

hooded, looking down at the cards he was packing into their case. He stood to return it to the games cupboard, carrying the writing pad and pen, as well. It prompted her to get moving.

Her hands shook a little as she collected the dirty glasses and took them out to the kitchen sink, her mind racing over what might be wrong. This was the first time they'd been alone together all day. She'd been waiting for it, half in dread, half in eagerness. Now it had come, Nick showed no sign of taking pleasure in her company. Quite the opposite.

She rinsed the glasses and left them on the draining board to dry, feeling driven to return to the living room and confront whatever was on his mind. Her heart fluttered with apprehension but she stuck to her earlier conviction. Better to know than not know.

He was standing, staring at the Christmas tree when she walked in. He swung around at hearing her and gave her a travesty of a smile. "Will you come out to the veranda with me? I don't want Kimberly overhearing us."

Meredith nodded and led the way, extremely conscious of him following her and closing the front door after him. When she turned questioningly, he waved her on to the cane armchairs where they had sat and talked the previous evening. He certainly didn't have making love in mind. Any desire he might be feeling for her was rigidly repressed.

It occurred to her he could be concerned that they had acted recklessly last night. Maybe he wanted to know if she was protected. In the heat of the moment, neither of them had considered consequences. Meredith supposed she should regret the carelessness. Somehow it didn't seem important.

He waited for her to settle in one of the armchairs, clearly too ill at ease to sit beside her. She saw his hands clench. He moved over to the railing, looking out to sea for several moments before turning his gaze to her.

"I know now that Merry was my special name for you," he said very quietly. "It was me you were speaking of when you explained it to Kimberly."

Shock rendered her speechless. He *knew*. She didn't have to tell him.

"Were you aware I had no memory of it?" he asked.

The pain in his voice squeezed her heart. Her mind was still in chaos, wondering how and when he'd realised this was not their first involvement. Nevertheless, it was paramount that she answer and answer truthfully. It was what she had wanted...to let him know. Though not for one moment had she anticipated he would preempt her in opening up the past.

She searched for appropriate words, delivering

them haltingly. "Your sister told me. She explained about your accident. Then last week, when you came about Kimberly, it was obvious you had no memory of me."

His hand jerked out in a hopeless little gesture. "I still don't remember."

That shocked her anew. "Then how...? I don't understand..."

"I called Dave today. Dave Ketteridge. He was with me that summer."

One of Nick's friends. She remembered them. The other one was called Jerry. Jerry Thompson. The three of them had been mates for years and obviously still in contact since Nick had called Dave today. Which meant he'd known he was Kimberly's father when he'd joined them in the surf, known all afternoon, all evening. It was amazing he'd hidden it as well as he had, waiting and waiting to get her alone without fear of interruption.

"Why didn't you contact me?" he asked, stress straining his voice. "At least, let me have the chance to...to..." Pent-up feeling exploded. "Damn it, Merry! It was my child you were carrying. I should have been told."

There was no way to avoid giving him pain and in justice to herself she had to tell the truth. "I did all I could to reach you, Nick."

"You met my sister." The accusation shot from him, carrying a load of anger and frustration.

"Yes. You'd left me her address. To write to you if I wanted to after a year had gone by. When I found out I was pregnant, my stepmother..." That was irrelevant. She took a deep breath and went on, concentrating on keeping her tone quiet and calm. "I caught the bus from Coff's Harbour to Sydney..."

"Your stepmother threw you out?"

Meredith winced. "Not exactly. Her sister said she'd have me if I worked in her florist shop. I was supposed to be coming to her in Sydney, but I went to your address first."

"And I wasn't there."

"No. Your sister said you'd been invited to go to Harvard and wouldn't be back for two years."

"You could have asked her for my address in the U.S."

Still accusing. Still critical. Meredith looked squarely at him and said, "I did. I was distressed. I made the mistake of telling her I was pregnant to you."

"Mistake! What do you mean 'mistake'?" he demanded tersely.

Meredith paused. There was no kind way of saying this. She sighed and recited the facts as they'd been put to her. "She didn't want your prospects of a great career ruined. She didn't want you coming home to a girl you'd forgotten, a girl who'd hang a baby on you when you weren't in a position to take the responsibility of it, a girl who wasn't old enough or accomplished enough to be a suitable wife. I'd be like an albatross around your neck.''

''She said that?'' He was shocked, horrified.

''I guess it was reasonable from her point of view.'' Meredith answered flatly.

''So what happened then?''

''I didn't believe her. I thought...she doesn't want me.'' She looked at him, her eyes aching with the memory. ''But I couldn't believe you wouldn't want me, Nick. I thought she was lying about your forgetting me.''

His chest heaved with a sharp intake of breath. He released it on a long shuddering sigh. ''It was true...yet not true. I dreamed of you. I dreamed of you so many times over the years, when I first saw you at your apartment...'' He shook his head. ''It's been driving me crazy.''

Enlightenment dawned. ''So that's why you rang Dave.''

''That and other things...things you said...the way I felt...''

Was he saying he felt the same as he had before? Or had that changed now, with harbouring a sense of betrayal since his call to his friend. He wasn't coming near her, didn't want to touch. His dark brooding didn't invite her touch, either.

Sick at heart, Meredith said, ''I tried to find

Dave, Nick. And Jerry. They were my only other leads to you.''

He stiffened. "Jerry knew where I was. I wrote to him.''

"There are five pages of Thompsons in the Sydney phone book,'' Meredith informed him. "I tried Ketteridge first.''

He frowned. "Dave went backpacking overseas that year,'' he muttered reminiscently.

"His father told me they were lucky if he sent a postcard now and then. The last one was from Turkey. It said Dave was heading for India. They knew you were in the U.S. but didn't have an address. I was given Jerry's home number.''

"And Jerry didn't help?'' Sheer incredulity.

"His mother answered the phone. She curtly informed me he'd moved away from home and she was sick of girls he'd left behind ringing him up. If he wanted to contact me he would. I managed to get in a question about you and she said as far as she was concerned, the same principle applied.''

He groaned and pushed away from the railing, pacing the veranda to the steps and back, then throwing out his hands in an aggressive appeal. "You could have tried a letter to Harvard University.''

The question cracked on her like a whip. Her head snapped up. "Could I, Nick?'' She pushed out of the chair to face him on a more equal level, her eyes blazing a challenge to his assertion. "I'd had every door shut in my face. Your sister said you'd forgotten me. Mrs. Thompson scorned me for running after you. It had been months since you walked away from me. Skipping out, my stepmother called it."

"I didn't," he swiftly defended. "It was for your sake I left."

"You weren't there to tell me that," she shot back at him.

"God damn it!" he exploded. "I still had the right to know."

"Rage at your sister then." Her voice shook with the emotional torment she'd been put through. "*She* judged for you. *She* knew you best. *She* made the decision."

He closed his eyes and rubbed his brow, shaking his head. "I'm sorry. I keep thinking...all these years...all these years... I should have been told."

"And I'm the only one you've got to blame. Is that it, Nick?" she mocked in a surge of bitterness for all the lost years.

"No!" His eyes flew open in a flare of anguish. His hand came down in a clenched fist, smacking into the palm of his other hand for emphasis. "I need to understand...to get the facts straight in my mind."

"To understand," she repeated derisively. She shook her head and swung away from him, moving over to the railing and looking bleakly at a sea that had been silent witness to her sorrows many, many times. "You couldn't imagine in a million years how it was for me."

A heavy sigh. "I do realise Denise has a lot to answer for," he quietly acknowledged. "I don't blame you, Merry. I just wish…"

"You think I didn't wish?"

He'd scraped the old wounds raw again, making her voice harsh. She swallowed hard and lifted her gaze to the stars, brilliant, distant dots in a universe of worlds that were unreachable. Like him, when she'd needed him most.

"I gave up my baby to your sister because she was your family, and at least you would know our child. And love her for me. But I still wished… I ached for you to write to me that next Christmas. As you said you would, if your feeling for me hadn't changed."

She turned to fling her own anguish at him, her heart throbbing with all the painful doubts and the painful decisions she'd had to make. "I didn't believe you'd forgotten me. But I didn't know if you wanted me. He'll write if he still does, I told myself. He'll write. And then I can write back and tell him about our baby. He'll come home and make everything right if he truly wants me. We'll be together."

Her passionate outburst hung in the air between them, the understanding he'd demanded weaving its stinging tentacles of truth, inescapable, devastating in their power to set his mind straight.

"But I didn't write," he said hollowly.

"No. And then I realised I really had given my baby up." The dead despair of that moment hollowed out her voice. "And there was no turning back the clock."

He said nothing.

An ironic laugh broke from her throat. "It haunted me so much, when your two years at Harvard were up, I went back to your sister's place, determined to see you. Just to see...had you forgotten or didn't you want me?"

"They'd moved," he answered for her. "As soon as Denise got the baby, they bought a new home."

Meredith's mouth twisted. "For all I knew she'd told you everything anyway. I was only hurting myself, not letting go." She shrugged. "At least she kept her word, sending me the photographs."

"Which eventually led me back to you." He sounded tired, spent, a long, long way from being happy about it.

Tears welled into her eyes. "I thought you'd come for me, you know? For a moment, when I opened the door to my apartment and saw you standing there...I thought you'd come for me."

"God!" He shook his head despairingly. "What do I say to you?"

That you love me. That you'll hold me tight forever and never let me go again.

Her whole body ached for him to say the words, to take her in his arms and press them home to her.

The click of the front door opening startled both of them out of their painful thrall. Nick spun around to see. Meredith watched in tense helplessness as Kimberly stepped out onto the veranda, a forlorn little figure, throwing anxious glances at both of them, uncertain of her welcome yet forcing herself to brave facing them.

"What are you doing out of bed, Kimberly?" Nick snapped.

"I couldn't sleep." Her voice wavered. "I got up to look at the presents again."

"Spy on us, you mean," he said grimly.

"Nick..." Meredith protested.

He flashed her a tormented look. "Kimberly has a habit of eavesdropping."

Meredith looked at her daughter, seeing her torment, too. "Did you eavesdrop, Kimberly?" she asked softly.

A grave nod. "I didn't mean to, Merry. The window was open and you were saying...saying..." She gulped and looked at Nick, her eyes huge and shiny with tears.

"Damn it, Kimberly! This is none of your business!" he thundered, too upset to realise how wrong he was.

It was her business. Kimberly had the right to know, too. Meredith watched in helpless dismay as in the artless, direct way of children, her daughter put the question straight to him.

"Are you my real father, Uncle Nick?"

CHAPTER SIXTEEN

TEARS rolled down Kimberly's cheeks but she seemed unaware of them. Her eyes clung to Nick in silent, desperate pleading for him to put things right for her. One of her hands was twisting the soft cotton of her T-shirt nightie, fretting at it in a subconscious need to hold on to something. Her hair, released from its ponytail, hung in a bedraggled fashion around her face. She looked like a lost waif, bereft of all that had had meaning to her, and Meredith ached to gather her in her arms and hug comfort and reassurance.

But it was to Nick her daughter looked for what she needed, and Meredith painfully held herself back from rushing in. She simply wasn't in a position to offer some secure platform from which they could all launch into a rosy future to replace the past. Nothing was really resolved between her and Nick. It was up to him to answer his daughter. It was up to him to answer all the questions now.

Yet Nick looked as lost as Kimberly, stricken by the realisation of all she might have overheard; the role her adoptive parents had played in taking her from Meredith, in preventing Nick from knowing about his fatherhood, ensuring he didn't link up with her mother again, and keeping the knowledge of her real parentage from her.

The world they had known had been torn up and the pieces couldn't be put together again. No matter what was tried, it wouldn't be the same. Couldn't be. The recognition of it made it all the harder to come up with the right thing to say. Or do. The moment had come upon them too fast. None of them was ready for it. Yet it was so important to get it right.

To Meredith, waiting on extreme tenterhooks, it felt like aeons before Nick moved. His face softened as he stepped over to the child waiting to be claimed by him. He squatted in front of her, his eyes on the same level as hers, and he took her hands, gently fondling them.

"Yes, I am, baby," he said softly. "I am your real father."

Kimberly bit her lips and shook her head, too distressed to speak.

"I didn't know, love. I didn't know until today," Nick went on. "But now that I do know..."

"How could you forget Merry?" It was a cry from the heart, carrying the sense that he'd let her mother down, let them all down.

The caring from her daughter moved Meredith to tears. *My child, fighting for me...* How quickly the bond had formed! Or had it always been there, waiting to be tapped?

Nick sucked in a deep breath, exhaling slowly as he reached out and gently smudged the tears on his daughter's cheeks. "I didn't forget her, Kimberly. I suffered a head injury soon after I left Merry all those years ago, and the weeks before the accident became a blank to me. I didn't remember meeting and falling in love with her, but I've dreamed of her ever since. I didn't know she was a real person. In my dreams, I could never reach her, but I felt if I ever did, she'd bring a special magic into my life. And she has. She's given me a daughter I didn't know I had."

More tears welled and overflowed, both from Kimberly and Meredith, though thankfully no one was looking at Meredith.

Kimberly swallowed convulsively. "Would you...would you have come back...and married her?"

"Yes." No hesitation. "I would have wanted to be a father to you, Kimberly. And as soon as I saw Merry, I would have fallen in love with her all over again."

Meredith's heart turned over. Was Nick expressing what he felt now? Or was he simply appeasing Kimberly's sense of rightness?

"Why did Mum keep her from you?" It was a

wail for what might have been. "It wasn't fair, Uncle Nick. It wasn't fair!"

Kimberly burst into sobbing.

Nick sprang up and hoisted her against his shoulder, hugging her tightly. She flung her arms around his neck and wept, her small body racked with the devastation of faith in the parents she thought had loved her, whom she had loved. Nick carried her to the closest cane armchair and sat down, cuddling her on his lap and gently rubbing her back.

Meredith could only stand helplessly by, waiting to give what assistance she could, when and if it was called upon. She fought a silent battle with her own tears, afraid she would distress Kimberly even more if she saw them.

Eventually the sobbing diminished to the occasional hiccup. Kimberly remained huddled against Nick's shoulder, limp and drained, accepting his silent soothing like a kitten, needing to be petted and loved.

"Kimberly..." Nick called softly. "What your Mum did was wrong. It was wrong for me and wrong for Merry. But she and your dad loved you very much. They didn't know how it had been between Merry and me. They thought they were doing the best for you. And they did, Kimberly. They did their best to give you a happy life."

Nick lifted his gaze to Meredith, his dark eyes anguished, apologetic, appealing for her understanding. She responded instantly, moving to crouch beside the child on his lap and rub her legs, chilled now from the cool night air and her enervated state.

"Kimberly...all the photographs your mum sent me year by year showed me a very happy child," she assured her. "I loved looking at them. As Nick told you, I have them all over the walls in my bedroom. Please don't let those years be spoiled for you now, my darling. You wouldn't be the wonderful girl you are if your mum and dad hadn't given you a very loving home."

A woebegone face peeked at her around lank strands of hair. "You would have loved me, too, Merry."

"I do love you. You're my own precious child. You always were and you always will be. Nothing changes that, Kimberly," Meredith promised her.

"But Mum took me from you. You said..."

"No. You've misunderstood, Kimberly," she broke in quickly. "I gave you to your Mum because she could look after you better than I could at that time. And she and your dad looked after you beautifully. Even if Nick had come back to me, I don't know if we could have done better."

Kimberly thought that over for a while before saying, "I would have had my real parents."

"You have them now." Meredith stroked the damp hair away from her daughter's pale little face, smiling as she tucked it behind her ear and said, "Aren't you the lucky girl, with two sets of parents loving you?"

There was a perceptible brightening of expression before a frown marred it. "You and Uncle Nick were angry at each other."

"No." Meredith shook her head, the smile still lingering on her lips. "Nick was upset because he couldn't remember and I was upset having to explain everything to him. But that's over now." She glanced up for his support. "Isn't it, Nick?"

"Yes. We've got it all sorted out, Kimberly," he assured her.

It stirred Kimberly into sitting upright so she could look Nick in the eye. "Have you fallen in love with Merry again?" she asked with disarming directness.

Meredith held her breath. Nick's gaze turned to her, telegraphing so many emotions they were difficult to decipher. A plea for forgiveness? Need for her understanding? Anguish at having been put on the spot?

"I never stopped loving her. Even when she was only in my dreams, she touched my heart."

Dear heaven! Was it true?

"Are you going to marry her now?"

The clear line logic of a child! It left nowhere for Nick to go. He was trapped within the integrity of what he'd already said in his efforts to soothe his daughter's distress.

His gaze did not leave Meredith's. It begged her response as he said, "If she'll have me."

Kimberly turned, her eyes full of hope and expectation. "Merry?"

She stood up, her legs trembling under the weight of decision. Two pairs of eyes were pinning her to a response here and now. Meredith's heart was pounding. She wanted to say yes, but was it right to do so when the question had been asked under duress? Did it matter? If Nick was truly willing for the sake of their daughter, why was she even hesitating?

"Yes," she said firmly.

Kimberly hurtled off Nick's lap and hugged her. "It's what I've been dreaming, Merry, for you and Uncle Nick to get married so I could have both of you all the time," she babbled.

Nick rose from the chair with the air of a man who had just had an enormous burden lifted from his shoulders. If he felt any weight from the responsibilities he had just taken on, it certainly didn't show. He oozed confidence, as though his world was under control again and what he had was what he wanted.

Meredith fiercely hoped so. She hoped she wasn't fooling herself into seeing what she wanted to see.

He gave her a grateful look and gently squeezed his daughter's shoulder. "Let's drop the uncle bit, Kimberly. Just call me Nick, as Merry does."

"Oh!" She swung around to beam at him. "Okay, Nick."

He tapped her cheek, smiling indulgently. "Off to bed, little one. It's Christmas tomorrow."

"And you and Merry want to kiss and make up," she replied with her own form of indulgence.

"You could be right about that."

She giggled.

Meredith was amazed at the resilience coming to the fore with the assurance of having both her real parents established in her life.

"Have a good night, Unc...I mean, Nick." Her grin was extended to Merry. "A very good night."

"Sweet dreams," Nick prompted.

"Yes. Sweet dreams," Meredith echoed, hoping her own dream was really coming true.

Kimberly walked jauntily to the front door, pausing before she made her exit to sweep them both with another grin, her eyes twinkling like stars. "Merry Christmas," she called very pointedly. Then off she went down the hallway singing, "I wish you a Merry Christmas, I wish you a Merry Christmas, I wish you a Merry Christmas and a Happy New Year!"

CHAPTER SEVENTEEN

As Kimberly's singing receded down the hallway, Nick's hands slid around Meredith's waist and turned her to face him. Her heart was fluttering so wildly she felt almost sick, apprehension and excitement warring inside her.

"Thank you," he said quietly, his eyes a swirl of dark chocolate, meltingly warm. "Thank you for being you, for having my child and giving her to me. But above everything else, thank you for waiting for me, Merry."

"Oh, Nick!" Relief gushed through her. The love in his voice was unmistakable. "I'm sorry I gave up on you. I…"

"No…" He placed a finger on her lips, hushing the stream of regret. "I was wrong. You don't have anything to answer for." The finger softly stroked down to her chin and dropped, his hand moving to curl around her neck and caress her nape. "God knows I've seen enough, been with you enough to appreciate, in some small measure, how it's been for you. I'm sorry I got so screwed up about being left out."

The fluttering eased. She managed a wry smile.

"Well, at least I'm not too young for you anymore."

He frowned, pained by the reminder. "I don't know that you ever were. Some feelings go beyond any sensible reasoning. Dave said if I'd had my mind on surfing, the accident wouldn't have happened. Maybe I was thinking of coming back to you and that was what the dream meant."

Twice he'd spoken of dreaming about her. Meredith's curiosity was piqued. "What happened in your dream?"

An ironic smile cleared the frown. "It was mostly like last night, you waiting on the beach for me, facing out to sea. You never spoke, yet I'd feel you were calling me. I'd set out to reach you and when I got close, you'd turn around as though you'd heard me coming and your face would light up in welcome." He sighed. "Then my legs wouldn't move any more. I'd stand helplessly, watching you fade away."

"How strange!" she murmured. "Sometimes, especially after a walk on the beach, I'd have a restless night. I'd lie in the dark, thinking of you, how I used to stand at the water's edge, watching you ride your board or windsurf. I guess, in my heart, I was calling to you, Nick."

They stared at each other, awed by the need that had spanned time and distance, calling from soul to soul.

Nick sighed, his eyes turning rueful. "I wish I'd known how to answer. But for Kimberly finding out about you and wanting to meet her real mother..."

"She's wonderful, isn't she?"

He smiled. "Very much like her mother."

"And her father. She's got your hair..."

"Your eyes."

She laughed, happiness bubbling up and brimming over. "Isn't it marvellous we can now be her parents? Oh!" She winced as the thought of Denise and Colin Graham hit her. "I didn't mean...I wasn't being glad about what happened to your sister and brother-in-law, Nick. It was just..."

"I know." He pulled her closer, warming her with his body. "It was good of you to say what you did to Kimberly, considering the selfish judgment Denise made."

"It wasn't entirely selfish," Meredith quickly protested, so happy to be where she was, nothing else mattered. "Your sister was thinking of you, wanting you to be a success."

He shook his head. "She was thinking of what *she* wanted for me, not what *I* wanted, Merry."

"Still, you've been very successful with your career," she argued, not wanting him to harbour ill feelings toward a woman who had given him and Kimberly so much. "You must be pleased about that. You like your work. I can tell."

"*You've* been very successful with your *Flower Power*. Did it make up for what we missed?"

She slid her hands over his shoulders and around his neck, her eyes earnestly pleading her case. "That time is gone, Nick. Let's not waste now in mourning it. And we've got so much to look forward to."

His face softened and suddenly broke into a grin, his eyes twinkling like Kimberly's. "You can take charge of the flowers for the wedding."

Her stomach felt as if it was twinkling. "Are we going to have a wedding?"

"We most certainly are," he answered with fervour. Then he laughed. "Kimberly would accuse us both of being stodges if we did her out of it."

"You really want to marry me?"

"Did you doubt it?"

Not now. The sense of coming full circle was far too strong. But it was fun to tease him, confident of a love that would go on forever, regardless of any obstacle or tribulation.

"Well, Kimberly did, more or less, force your hand," she said archly.

"Only getting to the heart of the matter more quickly, my love. And you are my love." His eyes searched hers with urgent intensity. "You don't doubt that, do you, Merry?"

She smiled, glowing with certainty. "You're calling me Merry."

"I wanted to before. It sounded right. Felt right. But I kept thinking it was *his* name for you and I didn't want you to associate me with the lover who'd let you down." He grimaced. "There's some irony for you."

"I'm sorry you don't remember, Nick, but it was the same as it is now. I never stopped loving you, either," she said softly.

"Merry..."

He choked up. His head bent. His lips moved over hers in a slow, sensual tasting. She felt his desire to savour every nuance of her physical reality and his intent to treasure the magic of this coming together. And it *was* magic, the touch of love, the sureness of it coursing through them, swelling their hearts and warming their souls.

With the deepening of their kiss came the need for every closeness, all the intimacy they had shared the night before, heightened by the joy of knowing the long yearning for each other was over. They were one again and the desire to express that in every way was too strong to delay.

"Share my bed with me," Nick murmured. "I want to be with you all night."

Blissful thought...yet they weren't entirely alone. "Is it wise with Kimberly? If she finds us in the same room in the morning..."

"It will cement her happiness," he answered

confidently. "She feels our marriage is long overdue."

Meredith sighed. "You know her better than I do."

He smiled, tucking her close to him for the walk inside. "You're catching up fast and you have the advantage of being female. Like minds..."

She laughed, sliding her arm around his waist and snuggling closer as they strolled to the front door. "You're good with her, Nick. I've loved watching how you are together."

He pressed a soft kiss on her temple. "She's part of you. I guess it shone through. She's always been a special child to me."

Special...

The sense of it sang in Meredith's mind and hummed through her body all during their lovemaking. Nick was special. Their child was special. The feeling they had for each other was special. And this wonderful Christmas had to be the most special of all.

CHAPTER EIGHTEEN

"I'VE got one more present to give," Kimberly declared, her eyes sparkling with the anticipation of surprising them.

Nick wondered what she had up her sleeve. They'd cleared the bundle underneath the Christmas tree. Three piles of gifts were now on full display, their discarded wrapping littering the floor around them.

"But there's nothing left," Merry pointed out.

Kimberly laughed. "I thought of it last night. You'll never guess."

"Are we allowed to play twenty questions?" Nick asked, happy to go along with the teasing.

He couldn't remember ever feeling so happy. The three of them were sprawled on the carpet in the living room, surrounded by the trappings and spirit of Christmas. It was a perfect day outside and everything was right with his world. Beautifully, wonderfully right.

"Animal, mineral or vegetable?" he tossed at his daughter, revelling in the knowledge of their true relationship.

"It's an idea, not a thing," she smugly announced.

Nick rolled his eyes. "Then I give up."

"Me, too," Merry said, shaking her head. "An idea makes it far too tricky."

"I knew you'd never guess," Kimberly crowed triumphantly. "I've decided to go to PLC as a weekly boarder. It'll give you and Nick lots of time together, Merry. Like a really long honeymoon. Just the two of you."

"Oh!" Merry flushed, still a bit self-conscious over Kimberly's pleasure in finding them together this morning. "It's a lovely thought, Kimberly, but is it what you want to do?"

"I don't mind at all now I know I'll have you both at the weekends. It'll be fun being with a whole lot of other girls, doing the same stuff."

"Sure about this, Kimberly?" Nick asked, touched by her caring for them, yet reluctant to lose the sense of family he felt so strongly this morning.

"Absolutely!" she replied decisively. "Merry can help me shop for the right clothes and I'll have lots of exciting things to tell you at weekends." Her brow puckered. "There's one thing though…"

"You can always change your mind," Nick prompted.

"No. It's Mrs. Armstrong. She's been really nice, minding me. I don't like the thought of putting her out of a job."

Nick felt a swell of pride in his daughter. The kind concern for Fran Armstrong showed a generosity of spirit that had been sadly lacking with Rachel. On the other hand, grandmotherly Fran was hardly a threat to the place Kimberly had secretly earmarked for Merry.

"Don't worry about Mrs. Armstrong, Kimberly. I'm sure we can come to some arrangement. I promise you she won't lose by it."

Relief spread into smile. "That's good. She's still waiting on a grandchild. Her daughter's been trying to have a baby, but no luck yet."

A baby, Nick thought, and looked at Merry, remembering their conversation earlier this morning. It had shocked him when he realised he hadn't thought of using any form of contraception. On both nights his need and desire for her had obliterated any normal consideration of consequences. It was Merry who'd thought of it afterward, asking if he minded if they had another baby. As if he'd mind!

She caught his gaze and the soft look in her eyes and her smile told him she was thinking of the same conversation. A Christmas baby. Like Kimberly. Though if it happened, he wouldn't be missing out on the birth this time. He reached out and took Merry's hand in his, squeezing it as he silently promised he'd be there for her. Be there for everything.

"I know!" Kimberly said brightly, drawing their attention. "Why don't you two have a baby? Mrs. Armstrong would love that."

The suggestion popped out so unexpectedly, it caught them both by surprise. "How would you feel about it if we did, Kimberly?" Nick asked.

"Really?" she squealed excitedly.

He laughed at her. "Yes. Really."

She clapped her hands. "I've always wanted a sister or a brother." Her eyes glowed at the prospect. "If you got to work on it straight away we could have a bigger family next Christmas."

Merry laughed, her cheeks burning even more brightly.

A Christmas family, Nick thought. What could be better?

"But you must promise to do all the baby shopping with me," Kimberly demanded of her mother. "I mean that's real mother stuff and I want to be in on it."

Her real mother...

Kimberly loved having her.

Merry was right. It was a miracle the three of them had come together and everything had turned out right.

He feasted his eyes on the very special beauty of the woman he loved and would always love. It was true. She made him feel as though all the Christmas lights in the world had been switched on inside him.

His Merry Christmas.

No. His and Kimberly's.

Their own special Merry Christmas.

Coming Next Month

HARLEQUIN PRESENTS®

THE BEST HAS JUST GOTTEN BETTER!

#1929 A MARRIAGE TO REMEMBER Carole Mortimer
Three years ago Adam Carmichael had walked out on Maggi—now he was back! Divorce seemed the only way to get him out of her life for good. But Adam wasn't going to let her go without a fight!

**#1930 RED-HOT AND RECKLESS Miranda Lee
(Scandals!)**
Ben Sinclair just couldn't put his schoolboy obsession with Amber behind him. She *still* thought she could have anything because she was rich and beautiful. But now Ben had a chance to get even with her at last....

#1931 TIGER, TIGER Robyn Donald
Leo Dacre was determined to find out what had happened to his runaway half brother, but Tansy was just as determined not to tell him! It was a clash of equals...so who would be the winner?

#1932 FLETCHER'S BABY Anne McAllister
Sam Fletcher never ran away from difficult situations, so when Josie revealed that she was expecting his child, marriage seemed the practical solution. And he wasn't going to take no for an answer!

**#1933 THE SECRET MOTHER Lee Wilkinson
(Nanny Wanted!)**
Caroline had promised herself that one day she would be back for Caitlin. Now, four years later, she's applying for the job of her nanny. Matthew Carran, the interviewer, doesn't *seem* to recognize her. But he has a hidden agenda....

**#1934 HUSBAND BY CONTRACT Helen Brooks
(Husbands and Wives)**
For Donato Vittoria, marriage was a lifetime commitment. Or so Grace had thought—until she'd discovered his betrayal, and fled. But in Donato's eyes he was still her husband, and he wanted her back in his life—and in his bed!

Harlequin Romance®
and Harlequin Presents®

bring you two great new miniseries with one thing in common—MEN! They're sexy, successful and available!

You won't want to miss these exciting romances
by some of your favorite authors,
written from the male point of view.

Harlequin Romance® brings you

Starting in January 1998 with Rebecca Winters,
we'll be bringing you one **Bachelor Territory** book
every other month. Look for books by Val Daniels,
Emma Richmond, Lucy Gordon, Heather Allison
and Barbara McMahon.

Harlequin Presents® launches **MAN TALK**
in April 1998 with bestselling author Charlotte Lamb.
Watch for books by Alison Kelly, Sandra Field and
Emma Darcy in June, August and October 1998.

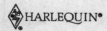 HARLEQUIN®   *There are two sides to every story...
and now it's his turn!*

If you are looking for more titles by

EMMA DARCY

Don't miss these fabulous stories by one of
Harlequin's most popular authors: